FOREVER & Beyond

Saumendra

PARTRIDGE

ISBN: Hardcover   978-1-4828-8651-1
             Softcover   978-1-4828-8650-4
             eBook   978-1-4828-8649-8

Print information available on the last page.

To order additional copies of this book, contact
Partridge India
000 800 10062 62
orders.india@partridgepublishing.com

www.partridgepublishing.com/india

This book is dedicated to

My sweet niece Gungun,
nephew Aayush and son Aadhrit.

Acknowledgements

To transform a thought and imagination into words and then make it available for others to read and absorb the entire theme of the story in the form of a book is not at all possible by the efforts of a single person.

Hence I want to express my gratitude to the following people without whose support and encouragement it would have been impossible to transform this book into a reality:

My readers and admirers who have a taste and hunger for this kind of storytelling and narration and have encouraged me from time to time for getting the best out of me.

My parents, Smt. Sailabala Nayak and Shri Upendra Nath Nayak for their love and support which had always been a great source of inspiration to initiate and continue the work.

My both Sisters Sujata and Seema and my wife Rupanjali have always been a stanchion of my work and encouraged me for building up the script and give it a pragmatic touch by staying close to reality.

I am also grateful to my son Aadhrit and my pet Kuttu for keeping me engaged as well as relaxed during the entire work on the book and they both acted as stress busters in releasing all the stress to focus and concentrate on the good work.

To my dear friends Shikha and Kanchan for continuously buttressing my effort in completion of the work.

To my Publisher friend Pohar, Marian and their entire team at Patridge publication Pvt Ltd for establishing this work and materializing it as a book of Supernatural Romance.

To my batch-mates, seniors and juniors at MANAGE, Hyderabad, MSU, Vadodara, College of Agriculture, Bapatla and Cambridge school, Cuttack for constant support and admiration of my work.

To my colleagues at Dhanuka Agritech Ltd, and my Ex-colleagues at BASF India Ltd for their support and encouragement.

Finally I would like to give all credits to my Grandparents Gouranga and Sundari and to God, the Almighty for their blessings to complete this book.

Prologue

We do not see oxygen, but we breathe

Certain things that we do not see, but still have to believe

We come across many things in life which we do not see but they exist like the air that we breathe in to survive, the internet, Wi-Fi and mobile signals that we use day in and day out, but we never touch or feel or see them.

Everything in this universe is maintained by a balance of good and bad, holy and evil, positive and negative. And these balances are sustained by desires to achieve and these desires are carried out in the timeless frame of universe in the form of emotions and feelings associated with those desires.

Human emotions are not bound by time and space which are the two most defying forces of nature. We, with the fear of losing ourselves in this vast universe demarcate time and space in this timeless and limitless space by assigning a number or a name to it like 1,2,3,January, London, Mumbai, Earth, etc. Just to identify our existence in this universe we demarcate ourselves against these two defying forces of nature i.e. Time in terms of date of birth, Anniversary, year of Graduation, and place in terms of Place of Birth, Place of work etc. If we leave any count of dates or do not identify any place by its name, then it becomes impossible to note our existence and we do not have any reference to say what we did, where we did and how we existed.

Hence there is no start or end to any process or event that happened in this countless time frame of unmeasurable universe where planets have been rotating, revolving along with their solar systems from unknown unmeasurable timeframe. Therefore emotions and feelings cannot be confined to time of a person's existence and do continue to exist beyond that.

It continues beyond days, months, years and ages which is why we sometimes feel it for someone and someone might feel the same for us even when anyone of us is not around. Which is why we remember and miss people even when we are continents apart or may be decades apart. We are not just remembered as events that occurred but also people feel the love, anxiety, anger, hatred and all sorts of emotions while thinking of someone.

So the human emotions particularly when longing for someone continues in this limitless and timeless frame of universe for ever even after the persons are gone. The only thing that needs someone to feel it is the emotional frequency of the receiver matching it.

Sometimes these emotions are so strong that they stick together and disapprove to dilute and disperse in this universe. They become stronger when we remember them and they are felt by us when we name them. When we deliberately try to forget them then we unknowingly feed these wondering emotions with our thoughts and they are drawn closer.

The only way to keep away from them is by the existence of some other positive emotions like love and affection which is stronger and is closer to us and we want it to overshadow other emotions and keep us indulged and engrossed in it.

The absence of Light is Darkness

The absence of Warmth is Chillness

The absence of God is Evil.

With the glow of light darkness vanishes. Similarly, only positivity can feel the void called negativity.

Contents

Journey Commence Through The Old Tracks
Of Memories... 1

Leap Of Faith.. 9

Unraveling The Truth At Vadodara 17

Knowing The Unknown.. 27

A Sweet Birthday Present 45

Inclination For Her At Vizag..................................51

Liquid Test Of Love 62

Surprises –Pleasant Or Strange? 76

Journey For The Quest Of Origin.............................. 86

Am I Ready Now For The Last Plunge? 104

Journey Commence Through The Old Tracks Of Memories

It was 15 past 11 PM and I was sitting on a bench on platform No.1 of Mariani Junction near Jorhat in Assam and waiting to board my train which has already been announced to arrive but was still not appearing on the tracks of the Station's platform. It was a normal chilled winter night of January but I was feeling the warmth of satisfaction of completing my official task that I was assigned at Tocklai Research station.

'Nisha…..Nis…. Don't run. Stay close dear.' Someone called her sweet little kid as she ran past me on the platform. This reminded me of someone with a similar rhyming name although I was not able to recollect anyone from my recent past.

Suddenly I observed someone at a distance who was obvious to attract my attention with her face which seemed to be much familiar, although I failed to recollect my memories of knowing her. She was clad in a black saree and had covered her head with a black scarf studded with star shaped twinkling golden dots that was reflecting the overhead lights.

My mind which was very calm and restful after the long hectic week of work and travel and was filled with a sense of satisfaction of accomplishment suddenly became restless and started churning out memories with an intension to retrieve any moments of my life that might have been associated with her.

With a sudden and harsh noise of blowing of horn of the iron monster- "The Train", my concentration broke and I grabbed up my suitcase and rushed towards the second AC coach of A1 and boarded the Kamrup express. The train was supposed to stop there for 2 Minutes and I was in a hurry to settle down on my berth before the train departs.

Once I settled down, then I started looking outside at the platform where the lady was occupying her seat, but could not find her. Now the strains on my eyes were really intense as I was trying to locate someone who seemed familiar although unable to recognize her and this half a minute seemed as if my last chance to rediscover her.

The train blowed its whistle; the TTE standing on the platform with the long list of passengers in his hand slowly walked towards the train and pulled himself into the train grabbing its long iron handles.

The train started rolling its big iron wheels slowly, while I became more and more desperate of finding her and even more fearful of losing her. Suddenly a soft voice interrupted all my efforts. 'Excuse me, that's my berth'.

I turned back my head and looked back into the train in a direction from where the voice descended. What I saw almost made me lose my senses for a moment and I did not respond to anything.

The voice repeated again softly, 'That is my berth. Would you please…?'

I nodded and stood up immediately; even don't remember whether my nodding meant "Yes" or "No".

It was the same charming and familiar lady standing before me for whom I had been scanning the entire platform till now as if I had left someone on the platform who had accompanied me and now not been able to find her when the train started moving ahead leaving behind the platform.

After a moment of silence, I finally reacted and said 'Oh yes, Mine is 18th' and she said 'yes, that's the upper birth. The one that you had occupied is 17th, which is mine.'

I did not recognize this till then and all of a sudden felt as if I am an idiot.

'Oh so stupid of me', I said and as I started gathering my bed roll, she suddenly stopped me by asking 'Are you "Sneh", I mean Snehashish?'

'Do I know you?' suddenly came out of my mouth as if these four words had been struggling a lot to eject from my mouth since last 15 Minutes.

She smiled radiating an energy and said 'Don't you recognize me? Myself Anisha. We were together in the same class and same school till 10th standard in Cambridge.'

My mind which had been scanning the entire universe for a memory particle that would suffice my quest, suddenly zeroed down to my school days from class 6th to class 10th and again went back to the fourth bench on the girls row onto my left and things started becoming more and more clear as if someone has zoomed in from the Google Maps.

Now things were clearer and I could see this silent, shy and dusky girl of my classroom turning into a vibrant and radiant lady gleaming full of energy.

I admitted by saying 'Oh yes, I do remember, but sorry I could not recognize you.'

Then I removed my bed roll from her birth and laid it on my berth, which was side upper (SU).

She laid her bed roll too on her berth. As I was about to climb onto my berth, she suddenly stopped me again by saying, 'Why don't we sit and talk for some time till we feel sleepy?'

The only two words that could have come out of my mouth at that moment, came without any hesitation. 'Why not?'

She invited me to sit beside her and I did so as if it was the only thing that I was supposed to do in the whole of the universe.

She asked me in a soft voice 'Where are you up to?'

I said 'NJP, New Jalpaiguri. Where are you going?'

'I am also going to the same place. So we have enough time talking to one another.'

She proposed to keep talking till we feel sleepy and I said 'Yes.'

This sweet silent lady of my class now initiated the talk by asking 'Where have you been?'

'Tocklai research station on some official work.' Was just wondering if she know about Toklai.

Suddenly she surprised me by saying 'Oh really! I work there.'

Then we started talking about our past school days. She had a brilliant memory and was able to recollect many things about me although I was unable to do so, especially about her. Only thing that I was able to recollect about her was that she used to be a silent, calm, descent, sober and sincere girl. And now I understand the reason why I am unable to recollect anything about her. Probably all these adjectives are sufficient enough in masking a person's popularity particularly when they are not known for higher or poor marks. She helped me to see again my childhood days with much clarity by removing the dust of time through her brilliant memories.

One thing I could make out from her memories and expression of those past time moments as if she was reliving those moments again and enjoying every bit of it. In my school days I was a jack of all trade and master of none. I got myself involved in all sports, was the house captain for 2 years for the entire school, actively participated in elocution, debate, quizzes and won nothing. I even didn't remember that she was in my house in the school of which I was the captain until she told me what a great inspiration I was for her as a house captain. I really wondered if she was complementing.

A third voice interrupted our talk and brought us back to present from those good old days of childhood and juvenile memories. But this voice was a bit harsh and it said *'So Jao, abhi raat ke ek baj rahe hain. Baki ka schooling kal pass kar lena. Pehle toh light off karo.'*

I suddenly sprang up into action and switched off the light. When I stood up and was about to retire, saying 'Good Night', she caught up my arm and said 'Wait for a few more minutes, we may not find the time tomorrow'.

In my mind I questioned 'Why not tomorrow?' we would be reaching our destination by 4:30 PM the next day. That means we have plenty of time to interact the whole day next morning. I remained silent and said nothing. We started talking again but with a caution not to disturb people around us in their sleep.

Only one thing that I noticed during the whole conversation was that although I was enjoying the conversation and reliving those childhood days, but my body was chilling and I could feel the chillness down my spine in spite of the temperature within the coach turned up to make people feel warm and cozy while sleeping.

She enquired about what I did all these years and when I started asking what she had been doing, she said 'You will come to know soon'.

Time was fleeing faster than the train and suddenly she stopped me and asked me to go and sleep although none of us was feeling sleepy. I turned on my mobile just to check the time and it showed quarter to 4 AM. I wished her 'good night' and went to sleep. I was just lying on my berth and still waiting to fall asleep when I again looked at my mobile by turning it on and found it was half past four in the morning. I looked down at her berth to check if she was sleeping, but could not find her on her berth. Thinking she might have been to the washroom, I lied down for a while. Then I tried to sleep putting my earphones in my ear with mild old melodies from Bollywood and this time I was successful and I slept.

When I woke up it was 7:30 AM. She was still not there on her berth. She was carrying a single airbag and that too was missing.

I reached Guwahati Station at 8:30 AM. I got down on to the platform to check the passenger list of our coach. There was no name mentioned against berth No. 17. We interacted for over 4 hours and none of us had exchanged our mobile numbers. This may be because I never thought she would disappear so suddenly just as we met. Might be she was travelling on a wait listed ticket which got confirmed after chart preparation, which is why her name does not appear on the passenger list.

But why would she not reveal her true destination?

Why would she lie to me?

Did she leave her berth between 3:45 AM and 4:30 AM?

If so then where did she go as the train never stopped in between?

Many questions – No answers.

So it is always better to forget such an incident as if it had never happened or else it will always keep hunting with many unanswered questions for many days. But was it really an end to a sweet dream or was it the beginning of a new chapter which is still unclear. Whether it is going to open up few new pages in my life or am I destined to lurk for the unanswered questions forever?

Questions kept shooting up my mind which was unable to answer even a single one out of those.

Leap Of Faith

Time passed and life does not take much time to get back on track as per the law of inertia. Three months had passed and after an immediate promotion, I had moved to a new location, the beautiful city of Amravati in Maharashtra which is regarded as the queen of Vidarbha and supposed to have tough and harsh summer similar to the tough customers of that market.

After 5 days of halt in Amravati in a hotel and able to find a house for myself on rent to reside, I thought of taking a short break on the weekend and planned out for Chikaldara which was quite near to my place and a silent hill station with cooler climate.

Chikaldara is a little explored and the only hill station in Vidarbha which has almost 35 Km of steep slope of motorable road to reach to the top of it. It is situated in the range of Satpuda and is graced with dense forest known to be the abode of many wild life, lakes waterfalls and ruins of an ancient fort of Gavilgarh. The beautiful deep gorges of the lush green hills unfolds an unwrapped mystery in itself which also offers the opportunity of walking through clouds. This place has its roots deep from the time of Mahabharata, where Bhima had Killed Khichaka and hence the original name was "Khichakdhara" which finally came to be known as "Chikaldara".

I was enjoying my evening drink at a lawn restaurant on that summer evening at the hill station, when suddenly a waiter approached me and asked me if my vehicle number ends with 8136.

I said 'yes. Why?'

The waiter politely requested 'Please change your parking place Sir, as it is blocking someone's vehicle from moving out.'

I immediately got up from my chair and moved with the bunch of keys that was lying on my table. I slipped into my vehicle, pulled on the reverse gear and parked it at another place. Then when I moved near to an old "black Santro" car, whose path I was earlier blocking. Suddenly a chilled breeze ran down my spine. I wondered the chillness as it was a pleasant summer evening and the temperature although low being a hill station, but was still around 20 degrees Celsius.

When I approached the car and was about to knock on the completely dark tainted glass, the glass rolled down and I was taken by surprise to see what I was looking at in the car. There was a bright smiling face radiating all the pleasantries and it was the same face that appeared without expectation a few months back then disappeared only to appear again without expectation. It was really a very pleasant surprise to me. She was Anisha again and in all her beauty, calmness and grace.

Raising my arm in a gesture, I said 'Hi….hhhhh, you here? I just can't believe this.'

She simply smiled and said nothing.

I felt really strange with her smiling face as if she was very much expecting my presence there.

'Hello', she said in her usual soft calm voice.

I don't know why but this time her voice seems to tell me many things although she did not speak any second word other than 'Hello' at that moment. After a brief silence, she invited me to the seat next to her in the front seat of her car. I took the offer, opened the door, sat down and buckled my seat belt. There was a strange but sweet fragrance emanating from within the car. The sense of silence continued and we maintained it as if we had agreed to do so, without any one among us proposing to do so. It was a moonlit night and the full complete big round moon as if blood red in colour was flooding all the area under its focus while she drove silently with some old melody from some Black & White movie featuring "Devanand" was being played from her stereo.

She drove the car for about 15 Minutes through the arduous turnings of the hill and I could see a very expert driver in her who could drive with ease on the hill with steep slopes and blind turnings where most expert drivers would have encountered difficulties to drive at night.

She stopped at a place which was peeping over other peaks of those hills. She turned her face towards me and gave me a decisive smile, pulled the hand brake and got out of the car. I followed her and came out too. A fresh breeze of air dashed against my face and I could feel her fragrance through the air. She stared at the full moon for a while and then raising her arm towards the moon, said 'Do you still remember those school days when we went for a picnic and as one of the rear tyres of the bus got flat with no spare tyres to fit, we had to get down and do camp fire whole night. It was also a moonlit night of full moon like this and was drenching the grass covered valley as if we were out to play in a garden in daytime.'

As she spoke of these words, I saw a glimpse of her desire as if she wish to go back to those moments and hold the time there.

I smiled and said 'Yes, that was in class 9 and it had been a long time.'

She looked at me and said 'You feel it was a long time ago, because you had moved on since then. But I haven't. I am still there very much. Are you willing to cross that barrier of time and space and go back to those good old times? If you desire so then come forward. I will take you there with me.'

I was confused by her words as she meant nothing to me and I could not find any meaning in them. Hence I asked her 'Are you there? I mean are you in your senses or simply uttering some words without properly meaning anything.'

Anisha looked at me with her beautiful deep eyes and said in a grave voice 'If you believe you can get back to those wonderful years, then step forward with your faith and jump over this cliff. If not then you are not yet prepared. Let's go back.'

Her words really sounded crazy to me and I was not able to believe what I was hearing to. Her eyes revealed some kind of mystery which I was unable to solve. So I went back and occupied the non-driver seat at the front in the car. I was still trying hard to understand what she had just said, while she drove me back to the restaurant. She dropped me at the gate of the garden restaurant from where we began and asked me to go in and wait till She Park her vehicle.

I did as per what she told but later realized myself to be such a stupid for not accompanying her to the parking lot, even though she was a lady. I kept on waiting at the table lying near a well decorated ornamental plant with a small burning lantern kept on the table.

15 minutes had passed and now I was worried about her since she was still not there with me. After enquiring twice from the waiter, I stood up and started walking towards the parking lot with a fear in mind of losing her again. When I reached the parking place, I could not find her vehicle with the number plate of Odisha ending with 8956. When I

enquired from the parking security, I was shocked to learn that there was no such vehicle with this particular number plate that entered the parking area nor did he see me getting down from such a vehicle. It was really strange but there was no point in arguing.

My mind was yelling loud 'You lost her again'.

But this time I was not much worried as I was sure to have remembered her vehicle registration number which would help me in tracing out her address. After getting back to my room in the hotel, the first thing I did was started looking for her vehicle number from the internet.

It was not much of an effort to "Google" out about her vehicle from the Registration number from the internet, but this is not what I was looking at. Really astonished to see many news lining up before me to be read with a feeling of reluctance curiosity.

I could not believe my eyes reading out a news from the web, which interpreted by my brain says that this particular number registered by Odisha's RTO belongs to a "black coloured Santro car which fell into a deep gorge from a hill after its steering wheel got jammed. The only girl named Anisha, who was driving the car, could not survive this accident. Although her body was never recovered from the forests of the deep gorge, but eventually declared dead after a period of 6 months."

A sensation of chillness ran down my spine and blended my emotions and fear with the curiosity to find more about her. In this age of social media, and self-revealed updates, I hardly thought of going to the local library to find her whereabouts from a pile of old newspapers graced with layers of dust, respecting the law of inertia. I thought of finding more on the Facebook- the best buddy of all moods.

I found her profile without much of an effort and although her profile was active but with no updates since last 1 year.

Then I landed up on another profile on name of Aakanksha who was the cousin of Anisha. I could find Anisha's photograph with her but my confirmation of fear was slowing turning into reality as I could not find any of Anisha's photograph with Aakanksha that had been snapped in the past 1 year. Facebook was kind enough to reveal that Aakanksha was pursuing her Masters in Biotechnology at M S University of Vadodara and this was not a place far off from mine where I can reach within 24 hours.

Can't say if my trip to Vadodara was destined or desired but I made up my mind to meet her in person only to unveil the curtains of anxiety.

Unraveling The Truth At Vadodara

Working for a MNC provides me the liberty of a long weekend as Saturday remains an off for me every week. I took a leave on the next Friday and started on a journey of imagination and curiosity where I was never sure what to anticipate.

It was an overnight journey and I took a luxury semi sleeper bus to Vadodara. Vadodara, a great city of warmth and hospitality was not new for me as I had visited this place earlier on business as well as college trips. I had a real good pal of mine who was pursuing his Ph.D from Vadodara and I took it as an opportunity to hang on with him rather than staying in hotel as I would relive some good old time memories.

On reaching Vadodara at about 6:00 AM I took an auto-rickshaw to my friend Bhargav's place. He was really delighted to see me after a long time. We simply had a guideless talk with no proper adherence to any topic and it started with our current appearance, to job, to family, study days, old crushes, present likings, boring lectures, sadistic pleasures of professors and what not. Just the kind of best buddy talk. Only topic which I did not utter was the reason why I was there. I simply said the reason of my travel was official since he would never believe if I say I was there to meet him.

Now he got ready for his Biochemistry lab and I also got ready for my quest of truth. Now I decided to meet Aakanksha at her department of Biotechnology. It would never be a problem in approaching her in her department. I was not sure about what to ask and what to know.

As I reached the department of Biotechnology, I found it quite idyllic place situated on the lovely banks of Vishwamitri River which flows right through the middle of the beautiful serene campus. The murmuring of the water of the stream can be heard from the Radioactivity lab on the ground floor. I came to know that Aakanksha is in her lab on the fourth floor. As I climbed up the stairs, I could see and imagine why almost all the students are so slim and healthy, reason being the pretty high steps on the staircase and good number of stairs to reach the fourth floor. I could also see a lot of cleanliness around due to continuous sanitization maintained for the experiments. As I reached the lab on the fourth floor, I asked for Aakanksha.

Someone else echoed her name to help me out and then what I saw was a fair, good looking girl with curls of dark black hair, swinging around her forehead and hands wrapped up in high heat resistant pair of gloves and an spotless milky white apron with sleeves up to her elbow, revealing the identity of a future scientist of the nation came out through the lab door.

Her beautiful pair of deep black and dazzling eyes although hid behind fashionable but studious reading glasses seems to be in a hurry as if she was in the middle of an experiment.

On questioning she said 'Oh yes, I was doing the autoclave.'

Without further wasting any time, I said, 'Myself, Snehashish from Amravati, a classmate of Anisha. I need to talk regarding her.'

Her eyes became more inquisitive and strainful as she asked me to wait since she was in the middle of an experiment and it would take her about another half an hour to complete. I told her that I will wait for her and would move around the beautiful campus till then as it is one of the most beautiful campuses carved out of an old palace from the royal family of Maharajas of Vadodara.

She asked me to meet at the canteen outside the department in half an hour.

I affirmed it.

Gujarat is famous in whole of the planet for one of its snack named "Dhokla" and I decided to relish it at the authenticity of the place while waiting for her at the canteen.

It was 20 past 10:00 AM when I could see a young girl who looked a slight different now from the regular scientist's kind of look whom I spoke to around half an hour back approaching my table in the canteen. Now Aakanksha was not having her colorless apron and also has got rid of her heavy studious spectacles and looked more approachable than a scientist in a lab or in a patience threatening seminar where we always feel as if our watches got stuck or are the slowest from the rest of the world.

On approaching my table, I offered her something to eat or drink and she ordered 2 coffees.

Before my mouth could utter any more words, she asked me 'How do you know Anisha?'

simply said 'She was my classmate in the school till 10th although sometimes in different sections and sometimes together, but we were classmates for 5 years till we passed out together from class 10.'

She spontaneously asked 'Are you Snehashish from Cuttack, who later moved on to reside at Bhubaneswar?'

I nodded and said 'Yes, but how do you know?'

She smiled and tossed her head from right to left as if she knew many things about me and was really waiting for me to come there someday.

'Coffeeeeee' uttered a voice as habituated by the trend of serving students in the canteen and put 2 cup of coffee on our table with a thumping sound.

I She did not speak for the next 2 minutes, nor did I. But her eyes were continuously asking why was I there asking for Anisha, although she seems to be contradictorily waiting for me.

Putting back the cup of coffee on the saucer, she finally broke the conversation of silence and asked me 'What brings you here?'

'Anisha'- a word that came out of my mouth but did not find a second word to follow it but was sufficient enough for Aakanksha to understand it.

I started after a pause and said 'I am looking for Anisha. Can you let me know about her whereabouts?'

Now she entered into a pause as if something has tied up her lips. Sipping her last drop of coffee and putting the cup down, she heaved in a heavy voice – 'she is no more.'

I felt as if I am in the middle of a desert where war has just ended and my brain declared as a winner against my heart, which was still not ready to give up. It was the fear of confirmation where I always wished to prove myself wrong. Suddenly all the noise of a University canteen disappeared from my ears and my senses betrayed me at that moment. I forgot all manners, did not say sorry, nor reacted a bit, even no exclamation of belief or disbelief.

She asked for the bill and then I came back to reality taking the bill from the waiter and paid it. She asked for my number and said we could talk later as she has her classes commencing in 5 minutes. I even forgot to ask her number. She went for her classes leaving me alone with uninvited information without knowing how to react and respond.

I went straight to my buddy's place and went to sleep without having any lunch. I was still not able to digest what I heard from Aakanksha.

'Was this the information for which I was looking someone to confirm? Then why am I not able to believe it?' Now slowly many questions started swallowing my mind one after the other and the most prominent one among them was 'Did I meet Anisha when she was alive or after her death?'

Other questions that started tormenting me were:

'When did she die?

If she is no more than whom did I encounter twice?'

'Why did she show up before me?

Why only Me?

And why now?

How come Aakanksha knows about me and what all things she knows?'

Although I was not sure about answers to any of these, I was confirm about one thing that I have lost my sleep and not sure for how many nights.

I simply laid down on the bed thinking about all these things and was not sure how many minutes or how many hours have past, when suddenly I heard a knock on the door. I opened the door and it was my friend Bhargav.

'Hi Ashish, How was the day?'

I tried really hard to respond with an artificial smile, but he could guess that something was not right. I simply said 'Yeah, Everything is fine. The day went well as planned.'

Although he could guess that something has changed from the time he left for his department to the time he returned, but since he did not want to force anything out of me, he said nothing.

In the evening we went out to some of our old hangout places like Sayaji Baugh, Dairy Den, and the local chai wala in front of the front gate of University etc. to refresh our good old memories. Finally the gala Gujarati dinner at the old Gujarati restaurant where we used to go earlier refreshed our memories and I felt a bit relaxed.

While walking down the street towards Bhargav's room, I slowly and unconsciously went back to those questions, which had taken a leave from my mind for a few moments only. I again got engrossed in deep thinking about the answers although Bhargav kept on sharing the golden memories of the past.

But before long, my thoughts were interrupted suddenly by the ringing of my mobile phone. It was an unknown number and I thanked God for it as it does not belong to my boss since it was a Saturday evening and this one call could have spoiled my weekend by compelling me to work on something official.

I picked up the call and said 'Hello', then waited for the caller to respond. After a short pause a soft familiar voice said 'Hi, this is Aakanksha. When do you plan to leave?'

I said 'Tomorrow. Why?'

Then she asked me 'Can you stay for one more day? I need to show you something.'

'But I have my tickets booked for tomorrow morning train.'

It was a sort of demanding voice from Aakanksha when she said 'I don't know what brings you here. But do stay for one more day and I am sure both of us have something more to share about Anisha.'

As if both of us were expecting something unusual to be discovered when we meet again, I said 'OK.'

Bhargav was still not sure about what was going on but was happy to learn that I was going to stay for one more day. The first thing that I did on getting back to Bhargav's room was applied my leave online for Monday. I was fortunate enough to work in such a MNC which offers the liberty of applying for leave online without having to guess the mood of your boss, nor have to face him personally while asking for an unplanned leave.

I cancelled my train ticket and booked my return journey on a luxury bus. Bhargav was happy as we talked on for quite long into the night and then I asked him to sleep as he does not have the habit of vamping at night. The thing that kept me awake at night and anxious throughout the hours of loneliness is the thought about what can it be that Aakanksha wants to share with me regarding Anisha?

Knowing The Unknown

Bhargav kept on sleeping as it was Sunday but my curiosity pulled me up from bed as early as 6 AM. I called Aakanksha and said 'Good Morning'.

'Very Good Morning' she replied and it appeared as if she is awake since quite some time. I asked 'So when and where are we meeting?'

'Let us meet at ISKON Temple at 8:00 AM.'

'Fine' is the only word which I said as I was well aware about all the places in Vadodara.

I just left a note on Bhargav's table saying 'I am going to ISKON temple and will be back by lunch time.' I felt it absolutely unnecessary to wake a hard working studious guy from his cozy warm bed full of dreams on a lazy Sunday morning.

I went to the ISKON temple and went straight up to the altars of lord Krishna and admired His so different personalities in so many different avatars. As I sat in the calm and tranquil premises of the temple I started wondering if Lord Krishna is also wondering what kind of personality would suit Him if He desires to have another avatar in this age of current days, when suddenly I noticed Aakanksha entering the temple, dressed in all white. She looked prettier than yesterday. Actually she looked prettier to me only today as yesterday my senses were masked by a curiosity called Anisha. I never felt that way anytime earlier as I did that day looking at someone. I was new and naive to that feeling but enjoyed it. Then I dared to disturb myself and raised my arm to waive at her only by gesture as I did not find it proper to shout her name out in such a calm premise of the temple. She smiled and came to me.

Aakanksha softly whispered 'Hello. Let's go for a "Pradakshna".'

I agreed and we both went for a "Pradakshna". I felt this very different to all those "Pradakshna" that I made earlier alone. Earlier I felt a sense of achievement in touching the starting point twice and my focus was on my relative speed compared to other entities revolving in similar pattern. But now the focus was more on the journey rather than on the destination. I felt more relaxed and overwhelmed with a sense of gratitude. I glanced her with a squint eyed vision and could see her in deep thoughts but with contradicting calmness in her gesture. After completing our "Pradakshna" together we sat at one place on the lush green lawn of the temple garden. She looked at me and smiled again.

'What are your plans today?' (Aakanksha asked me without trying to restrict her smile).

I replied 'Now you have to tell me as I cancelled my tickets on your saying.'

She smiled and said 'I thought what we discussed yesterday was not sufficient and it would be an injustice if we do not talk more about Anisha.'

I nodded and replied 'Yes. Even I was not satisfied to go with half known information and also desired to share something unusual that was happening to me again and again these days which I have not yet shared with anyone till date. And what is that unusual I will tell you may be after sometime.'

'So what brings you here?'

'I came here to know about Anisha.'

'But why from me? And how do you know me?'

'I know about you from the "Facebook" profile of Anisha. Someone who has written a testimonial as if writing about someone whom she knows as much as herself, gave me a confidence that only you would be able to share real facts.'

She kept on firing as many questions as possible.

'But why now after so many days?'

I continued. 'Let me narrate the entire series of incidents that occurred to me recently.'

I narrated the battery of incidents which occurred to me in the form of an enigma called Anisha, right from meeting her the very first time in a small Railway station called Mariani Jn. and how she disappeared after talking to me for over 4 hours in the train and then suddenly one evening she appeared again out of the thin air outside a restaurant in Chikaldara, then drove me up to a peak among the hills and asked me to jump down the hill and when I denied then she again vanished after dropping me back at the restaurant where she had picked me up.

Then I told her that 'this event lead me to search about her on the internet and finally after all the things that I went through on the net I zeroed down to this place looking forward to you, Aakanksha as a source of information.'

I really could not believe myself speaking all these and wondered if the person whom I met for the second time only in my life would ever believe to what I was saying. I was totally clueless about how she would react and what she would say after hearing all this.

'She has come back.' These four words that she uttered confused me more as I was not able to decipher to what I was hearing.

She again repeated 'She has come back. She had told that earlier and she did.'

'What do you mean?' I asked as if I was pretending to be ignorant to the language she was speaking.

She spoke in a fearful voice 'She is not here but still she is around.'

I was really not able to believe to what I was hearing and hence I asked again 'Do you really believe in what I said or simply trying to pull my leg?'

'I know her as much as she knew herself.'

'But why me? Why only me? I mean why did she show up only before me and that too twice?'

Aakanksha got up from her place and said 'Come with me. I will show you why.'

So we walked again up to the lord, bowed down before the divine deity and moved out of the holy premises. We caught an Auto rickshaw and she asked him to give us a ride to the ladies hostel in front of Sayaji Baugh.

As I sat beside her in the back seat of Auto rickshaw, I could see an array of emotions on her face like restlessness, anxiety, curiosity and all these contradicting with a gentle smile on her face.

As I got down from the auto rickshaw in front of the ladies hostel, I was sure enough that this was the place in whole of Vadodara where you could experience a sense of pride when you go about to drop someone or pick up someone when your parents or relatives do not stay in the same city or else you could feel a sense of fear that someone might notice you there and when you open the door of your house, there will be your parents or guardians waiting in the living room to get an explanation from you.

I had been there earlier and the least price that you have to pay for being there is the cone ice cream priced at a premium by the hawker as he is well aware that no one can deny or bargain on this as it would cost them their date or even a relationship. I was fortunate enough that day as Aakanksha was neither my date nor the hawker was present there being it a Sunday morning.

I waited at the hostel gate as Aakanksha went towards her room asking me to wait for 5 minutes. I did not had to wait for long as she came out even before 5 Minutes were over and was holding her laptop in her arms. She booted her system and showed me a collection of items of which she had taken snaps. Anyone might have laughed or thought she might be kidding when she showed all the photographs in the folder.

But surprisingly I could not laugh as I found many of my lost articles from school in those photographs. I could see my kerchief which was a white one with the alphabet "S" embroidered on it by my mother so as not to lose it in school. But I lost it when I was in 7th standard. Also among them was my half knocked school batch which I had thrown and taken a new one in class 9th. There were also few things among those photographs which I never understood like an old eraser, a broken pencil, a cap less ball point pen, sharpened wood dust of pencil, and a key less ring.

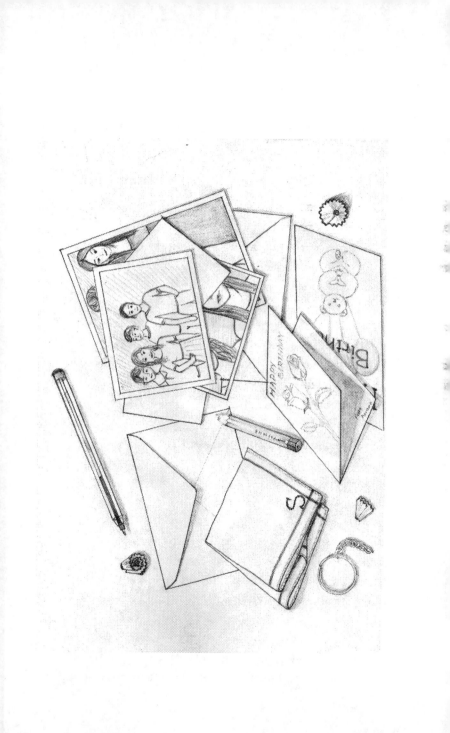

Aakanksha smiled and said 'these all were yours at some point of time either taken or stolen from you by Anisha not with the intention of stealing but with the purpose of possessing them as some prized entity in your memory.'

Aakanksha also showed me few greeting cards which had been addressed to me on my name but were never handed over. They were on various occasions like Diwali, New Year, Valentine's Day and my Birth Days. She also handed me a bunch of letters which Anisha wrote to me on her each birthday, but never posted them.

I was really becoming speechless with each discovery and struggling to find words that would describe my feeling. Suddenly Aakanksha told me not to speak anything before I go through all those letters. She also insisted that I should go through each one of them thoroughly and reflect on what I feel and try to relate all the incidents from my past school life if I remember anything about them.

'Fine' – the only word that came out of my mouth after all those things that I had seen.

Both of us understood it was time to say bye to each other. At least we now have the phone numbers to be in touch and hence said nothing and moved on as if we both have said enough without speaking much.

When I reached hostel, Bhargav was well awake, taken a shower and was busy with his Facebook and LinkedIn buddies as many would be available on a Sunday noon. On seeing me entering the room he smiled and said 'Hi. How was the day? You on a Sunday morning in a temple? Must be some "Devi Darshan" on the agenda!'

I simply smiled and said 'Oh yes. But…..'

Bhargav interrupted me by saying 'So many Love letters on meeting someone for the second time?' (Pointing at the bunch of letters in my hand).

'Actually these are not from Aakanksha.'

Bhargav replied (Shutting down his Laptop) 'Man I could smell some nice aromatic Khichdi, only does not know its ingredients. You met someone for the first time, but never took her number as if not willing to meet her again. Then rescheduled your ticket to meet her again. Then she meets you second time on a Sunday morning and that too in a temple. (He meant, actually people meet in restaurants or park or Multiplex). Then she hands over a bunch of love letters to you only on the second meeting but now you say those letters are from someone else! To me these are more complicated than riddles and crosswords in a Sunday newspaper.'

'Let's go for lunch because you need plenty of good food to digest all the stuff that I am going to share.'

Together we went for Lunch and had a sumptuous meal with special "Sev Tomato" and "Gujarati Kadi". Then we decided to go back to the room to rest.

I went through a couple of letters while lying down on the bed. I could not realize the moment when I entered into a good nap while traversing through old memories being refreshed by those letters.

Suddenly someone woke me up from my dreams and when I reluctantly opened my eyes it was Bhargav standing before me. He asked me to get up and narrate the story.

I suggested 'let's go out for a walk in the fresh air.'

On our way to Sayaji Baug, I told Bhargav that I came here to enquire the whereabouts of one of my old classmate Anisha from the school, from her cousin Aakanksha who is pursuing her Masters here. 'On coming here, I only realized that Anisha is no more but then I came across a bunch of letters handed to me by Aakanksha which were written by Anisha but were never posted.'

Bhargav was really sorry for what I said regarding Anisha and did not ask much.

We reached 'Sayaji Baug' and it was a lovely place in Vadodara and obviously the largest park and garden where people come to jog, walk, sit idle and spend time with someone you know or would like to know. In fact it was the best place in the whole of Vadodara to know someone whom you don't.

While looking at various phases of life in the same park, right from toddlers who have just started walking and their parents have brought them to enjoy those first baby steps to children who are busy playing and have started to understand the essence of teamwork and are deeply engrossed in games as if these games will be the basis of their future. We also observed the college goers who were trying to impress and woo someone as there would be boyfriend or girlfriend. We also could see the next phase of new love where it does not matter if someone is around and the whole world cease to exist when they keep their eyes glued to the most attractive marvel of the world (according to them). There were also newly-weds trying to enjoy all the infrastructures of the park and the couples who have been together for a long time and enjoyed a good time with each other and now trying to revive those sweet memories again.

The park also welcomes a good lot of calorie conscious and health conscious people who come for jogging or walking and consider all other people who are not there for the same purpose as unfit, unhealthy and simply wasting time. There were also some senior citizens who open the floor for discussions of all current affairs right from politics, sports, inflation to their family problems and take it with a pinch of flavor added for the taste.

While relaxing over the green soft carpet of grassy lawn of the park and observing all the phases of life together, I suddenly noticed Aakanksha with another girl, may be her roomie, just walking down the other end of the lawn. I raised my arm and yelled her name making her notice us and stop. Now Bhargav was well aware of the girl I called and accompanied me to go near her.

On reaching them I said 'Hi. This is my close buddy Bhargav.'

Aakanksha smiled and said 'Hello. Hi Bhargav. Let me introduce my roomie, Taashi.'

Both Bhargav and I greeted Taashi.

I said 'I will be moving back tomorrow.'

Aakanksha asked in a low voice 'Tomorrow morning?'

'No. I did not get a confirm reservation on train. Hence booked it on Volvo for tomorrow night.'

She reacted 'Oh'

Suddenly Taashi proposed 'Why don't you people join us for a few rounds of "Panipuri"?'

Bhargav was prompt enough to accept the offer 'Why not?'

Then we all proceeded towards the gate of Sayaji Baug and relished the Vadodara special "Panipuri" with a tinge of sweetness blended to sourness. After parting from Taashi and Aakanksha at their hostel gates, we proceeded towards Bhargav's room. On reaching the room Bhargav planned for a movie at INOX and although I had my own curiosity in going through all those letters, but since did not wish to disappoint Bhargav, I said 'Yes.'

Ongoing to INOX, we picked up our choice of Burgers and booked the show from 7 to 10 PM. Although the movie was a good one-time-see, but my mind was churning out something else. Suddenly I sighted someone sitting 3 rows ahead of us with a black scarf round her neck and looked very much like Anisha. While I was anxiously staring at her to confirm her identity, she turned back once and gave me a smile. I was about to get up and call out her name, suddenly there was light. It was the I-N-T-E-R-V-A-L. When I looked back at the same seat, I was surprised to see someone else on that seat with a beige color T-shirt. I did not feel like discussing anything regarding this with Bhargav.

We reached the room after the movie and it was time to go to bed. But I asked Bhargav to allow me to put on the table lamp so that I can complete some pending office work and I suggested him to go to sleep as he has to go for his classes the next morning.

Although I pretended to do some office work, but soon opened the bunch of letters when I found Bhargav in deep sleep.

There were 11 letters in all and each of them was written on each of her birthdays since she was in 8th standard. All the letters were addresses as "Dearest Sneh". While going through all those letters I could find a pattern. Till 10th standard many things which I knowingly or unknowingly did were mentioned in those letters. My participation in sports, literary competition and several events without winning a single one among them was mentioned in those letters although I thought no one has recorded those. I could sense a smell of enviousness in her words where she has mentioned me talking to her close friends.

From her age of 17th onwards when I was no longer in her class after the school, she still had gathered some information regarding my whereabouts and what I was up to. But now these letters seem to contain a lot of emotions of her and those happiest and saddest moments of her life which she had shared with me in those letters of her.

While the last letter of her was in front of my eyes, the table lamp started blinking and I had to put it off thinking that the voltage was fluctuating. I looked at the time on my mobile and it was 10 past 3 AM. I went onto the bed and closed my eyes. Who can ever sleep on that night after reading that emotional outburst? I simply lay down on the bed and waited for the sleep to devour me, which I believe happened around somewhat morning 5 AM.

Next morning Bhargav did not wake me up while going for the classes as he might have sensed the time when I slept. I still had one complete day as my bus was scheduled to depart at 8 PM in the evening. After going through all those letters I felt as if I should share with someone, but with whom?

At around 9 AM Aakanksha called me up and asked if I can meet her today if not bound by any other obligation. I said 'yes' since I had no other plans chalked out.

We met once again at the University library and it was a great place to be there whether you study or not. Some people go there to study, some to show that they study and others to see others study. Group study is decided not on the basis of the toughness or complexity of subject but on the basis of partners who opt to study together.

We both choose to sit on the chairs across a long table which was comparatively crowded as the people on the crowded table get less distracted and disturbed since everyone is busy in their small world and need not peep out of their world to see who else is occupying a seat in that table next to them. Whereas in lonely tables people attract the attention of everyone else in the library including the person sitting on the monitor connected to the CCTV and everyone watches with curiosity as if you are an alien about to do something unusual.

As we both kept staring at others, old books on the racks, huge magnificent dome of the ceiling and the old noisy creaking fans, both of us drew conclusions that we do not have much to share. Breaking the silence she said 'I knew about you since a long time.'

'How come? I just met you day before yesterday for the first time!'

She smiled and said 'Through Anisha. She shared everything with me including her feeling, emotions and what not. You might have read all those letters by now and understood her feelings from those letters. But for me she was an open book and I could read all her emotions even before she penned it down in her letters.'

I just kept listening......

Aakanksha continued 'She was madly in love with you and always used to say although you were unaware about her feelings but one day will come when you will understand her and her feelings and will respect her emotions. Today is the day when you know her as much as I do, but she is not there to realize how much you understand her feelings.'

Aakanksha's feelings were reflecting in her tears that were confined in her dazzling eyes which she never permitted to roll down. I don't know what to say although confused about my encounters with Anisha in the last couple of months. I asked Aakanksha if we can move out as I was feeling very uncomfortable without any single book placed before us on the table. She also felt uncomfortable on realizing the same and we both moved out of the library and went on to the beautiful green grassy lawn outside the library.

Then I said 'You would never believe me if I say I met her twice recently.'

'I will. I believe you as she used to say, she would never stop following you even when she is gone. Now I fear she is back.'

I asked anxiously 'Do you really believe in this?'

'Yes and you should also believe in her presence around you when you feel so. I know much about you almost in detail as if you were in my class and this is because Anisha used to narrate every detail of yours. When Anisha was no more I thought I would never be able to meet you in person, in spite of knowing so much about you. In fact I had built an image of yours in my mind and hence thought I would miss not only Anisha but also you.'

'So did you find me as per your imagination based on what Anisha had described?'

'Yes, but I found you a bit less talkative. May be you are not that comfortable with me as I am since I know you from last 11 years where as you know me only since day before yesterday.'

'May be I will speak a little more next time.'

'May be we are not meeting again.' She said smilingly.

'I don't think so. Things do not seem to end here.' (I don't know why I said this.)

We both parted with lot of things shared and with a hope to meet and share things again. In the evening when I boarded the bus I was still confused if I had achieved the objective of being there, but was much convinced that I had opened up a new chapter of my life while trying to conclude an old chapter of which I was sure that it had not been concluded.

As I laid my head against the comfy headrest of the Volvo, I was in a calm mood which was either after a storm or was about to enter into turbulence of a still severe storm that was fast approaching.

A Sweet Birthday Present

Sweet moments turning into memories flew as usual on the swift feathers of time and I got myself busy again in my routine official job until suddenly on a silent Saturday morning, when I was planning to sleep a little longer someone rang my door bell. I got up and unwillingly dragged myself out of the bed and pulled myself up to the main door. On opening the door I was angry enough to see a guy standing with a bouquet of purple orchids since I was damn sure that he would now ask me someone else's address as there was no one who would send me a fresh bouquet of Purple orchid although they were my favorite.

'Yes' I uttered in a casual voice.

'Mr. Snehashish?' he asked.

'Yes' I said again but this time with a voice filled with lot of thrill and excitement as no one had ever sent me even a blade of grass earlier.

Delivery Boy forwarded the bouquet towards me and said 'This is for you sir.'

I thanked him and on bringing the bouquet in, I found a note in it saying 'Many may happy returns of the day Ashish. Best wishes – Aakanksha.'

It was my birthday and I had forgotten it totally following a very hectic week at work and switched off my mobile last night after 11 PM so that no one could disturb me on a weekend morning.

Now I remember my parents and both my sisters who would have been trying since yesterday midnight for wishing me. I rushed to switch on my mobile phone and as soon I switched it on, the fine calm morning on a Saturday, matured into a noisy day with lots of messages wishing me on my birthday being delivered in my inbox, Facebook and WhatsApp. My parents and sisters called me and first expressed their concerns for finding my phone switched off before wishing me on my birthday.

Among all those wishes and complements, I forgot to thank Aakanksha for those beautiful flowers. In the evening I remembered to call Aakanksha to thank her for her wishes and those mesmerizing orchids. I could not believe that I kept her waiting anxiously for my call and it was so mean of me not to call her back since morning and thank her. She asked me about how did I spend my day and I was true enough to say that her wishes made my day.

I kept on speaking to her for about an hour when suddenly I heard my door bell ringing. I asked her to hang on as I went to open the door. When I opened ….. I found no one. On narrating what I found, Aakanksha said 'it was Anisha.' She was very sure as she also heard the doorbell. On asking how she could be so sure about it, she replied that she heard the clattering of her bangles and the "rumjhum" sound of her "payal", from the other side of the phone, when I opened the door.

Aakanksha continued saying 'her "payal" were special and I remember the sound well as I gifted it to her.'

I immediately shut the door and was getting goose bumps on hearing this. Suddenly the power went off and I could not hear any more voice from the other end of the phone as I kept on saying 'Hello, hello .. Aakanksha… you there?'

Strangely my phone got switched off. My confusions mounted with curiosity to know whether it was a coincidence or an accident. Now I lit up the candle and went for dinner. Although I was having the dinner all alone in the room but was ever feeling as if someone else was also there beside me on the dining table although not having dinner with me.

I even became more confident on my assumptions when the cool evening breeze coming through my window was not able to blow off the candle as if someone else was obstructing its way up to the flame. It was a strange feeling since it was not really scary but the feeling of someone sitting beside me and watching me while I was eating.

Slowly I kept on eating my meal and then went onto my bed as the electricity was still out and I was not cozy enough in the warmth of a candle on a windy night. I went to bed with mixed emotions of feeling good for the wishes I got on my birth day and the strange wrap up of the same day evening with a mysterious visitor who seems familiar.

In the morning I woke up only to notice that all the lights in my flat were on. I immediately checked my cell phone and found it to be functioning. After reading my way out through all the remaining wishes of my those friends about whose habit of vamping is well known to me, the first thing I did on my cell phone was called up Aakanksha and found her even more confused and worried as she was unable to reach me since last night as my phone was switched off since then. After speaking with me for a few minutes she got herself much relaxed.

Now she also mentioned her plans for Vishakhapatnam on the 5th of next month and asked me if I could join her although this was something quite unusual for me to be with her at a place somewhat around 1500 km from my city. She also mentioned that her expectations of me joining her in this trip were low as there seems to be no purpose for me to be there in Vizag. It was pretty evident from her voice that she was not confident of providing me a good reason to go to Vizag only because she was planning to go there.

I did not say anything while the beautiful rocky beaches of Vizag flashed onto my mind. But she took my silence as a negation and I also kept quiet. Unable to show my real interest of meeting her no matter whatever place be it,

I started scouting for a reason to be there with her. Also I could not dare to tell her that I would come to meet you and that is the only purpose. I started looking for a reason for the world and not for myself as I was clear about my purpose of visit. The reason for me being there should be able to convince Aakanksha as well.

I just booked my tickets because I knew Indian Railways would not wait for a reason and I have no reason to convince it or else I would land up on a waiting list. I kept on my quest for a reason and suddenly one fine morning I found one on Facebook. One of my close batch mate during my B-school days, Venkatesh popularly known as Venky was from Vizag. He was the most admired, respected and jovial guy of our batch, and the reason was the same as you all could guess- he was good at all things except studies. In one of his posts on Facebook he had invited anyone who would like to come for celebrating the 40th wedding anniversary of his parents.

No matter whatever the reason may be but now I have a valid reason to be in Vizag although I had booked my tickets earlier. But again in corporate life no matter how valid or genuine a reason look, it does not qualify in front of your boss especially when you are new to the organization. But I was fortunate enough to work in a company which allows me to apply for a leave online even with an option not to mention the reason.

It was 3rd of October, my tickets were ready, purpose was socially valid, leave was approved and Venky was informed of my visit. Now the most important task was still remaining.

I called Aakanksha to say that I too would be there for her at Vizag. I guessed she would take it as a pleasant surprise. But girls are known to surprise the surprises. She started complaining me about why I had not informed her earlier as she had already boarded her train for her seminar at Vizag and she could have grabbed her lemon-yellow color suit only if she could have known that she would meet me as she remembered me complimenting someone in lemon-yellow suit at Sayaji Baug and her friends say she looks prettier than anyone in that color of suit. Now you can never tell a girl why she looks beautiful and why actually you are attracted to her and she always concludes her apparels and jewelry worthy of the praise.

Whatever be her concern now the only thing that affected negatively for not informing her earlier was that she cannot postpone her journey and have to adjust the limited time between her guide, friends and me. The motivation of objective of a journey gives you the strength to endure and bear the length and time with patience.

Inclination For Her At Vizag

Aakanksha reached Vizag on 4th of October in the evening and had a plan to attend her seminar on 5th and 6th October so that there is one day free for sightseeing on 7th and finally her train to depart on 8th morning. I reached Vizag on 5th evening and although knowing that she would be free only on 6th evening from her boring seminars, but since I did not want to lose a chance to meet her even if for an hour and even if that meant travelling for one day in advance or staying back for one more day after the purpose. But I was fortunate enough as my visit to Venky's place was scheduled on 5th of October and I could make myself completely free by 6th October.

It was a wonderful time that I had with Venky and his family and although I pledged to have come there for attending the marriage anniversary as the sole purpose and even was able to convince Venky's family but Venky was wise enough to guess my purpose of travelling there purposefully.

On the evening of 5ᵗʰ October, Venky was kind enough to drop me at the gate of the hotel where Aakanksha was staying. Now I found myself really confused standing before Aakanksha while she was thanking Venky for being there and taking a lot of strain to come there. I spoke to Aakanksha for about an hour after Venky left us alone. But surprisingly Anisha did not appear in any of the topics of our discussion that day. Does it mean that we have moved beyond Anisha and now it is only between Aakanksha and me? Don't know the answer at the moment. I parted from Aakanksha, wishing her sweet dreams and with a commitment to meet her next evening.

Next morning I reached Venky's home from my hotel room to know more about Vizag and more particularly about those places where I can take Aakanksha for sightseeing. Also I involved Vandana Bhabhi in the discussion seeking her advice on this topic as she too had spent a great deal of her childhood days in Vizag. Venky winked at me with a gesture to ignore her advice as that would cost me dearly since most of the advice was around shopping and eating out.

On the evening of 6ᵗʰ October I again met Aakanksha and we went out for a dinner. This was the second most beautiful evening with wonderful moments that were about to turn into memories and I did not want to name it anything as I feared that it would limit the pleasure and bliss that I would derive from those moments spent with her. Before parting on that night, I gave her a choice that I would not compromise on her sightseeing, but only thing she needs to decide is whether she wants to go with her friends or with me alone.

This was a great gambling for me as my relationship which was about to take off was entirely on stakes with this choice that I gave her. Although I was confident enough on what she was about to say but still there was a latent fear hidden in some corner of my heart constantly poking me if I had done the right thing. Since I had already said that by then, there was nothing more to think or say before she actually replies me on this choice thrown to her.

Aakanksha smiled and looked into my eyes for a moment and then she replied 'So what time do we begin tomorrow?'

I thought of thanking the good Lord and Aakanksha for this, but I cannot do that openly, at least before her. We parted after deciding to meet at 7AM, the next morning.

Next morning I was in front of her hotel at five to 7 AM and found her waiting at the reception of her hotel, keenly looking at the entrance from where I would enter. Now I too was much excited looking at her interest for being with me and do not want to bother my mind to decide if her interest was for sightseeing or for the companion with whom she would be there for the next 12-14 hours for the sightseeing.

We started from the hotel just as planned, exactly at 7 AM. Now although she looked quite curious to know what all places were there on our agenda, but still she managed to maintain her silence as if we both had chosen the language of silence to communicate our feelings and she did not intend to interrupt the communication, nor the feeling.

We had some of the most beautiful, scenic and serene places on our list in and around Vizag but what was more exciting for me was being in the company of Aakanksha, which I was enjoying. We visited the marine museum, RK beach, Kailash Giri, where we even enjoyed the toy train ride and took our first selfie together at the foot of lord Shiva and Gouri. Also enjoyed the scenic view of entire city and sea together from top of Kailash Giri with the help of a telescope mounted atop the hill.

Towards the evening, we proceeded for "Dolphin nose" beach and finally saw the sunset on one of the most beautiful and romantic rocky beaches of Vizag which almost refreshed our memories of an evergreen romantic movie of Bollywood –*"Ek duje ke liye"*.

On one side of the beach we had beautiful hills with huge boulders and green vegetation while on the other side our feet were washed by the small tides of the sea. We kept on walking along the shore looking at the Sanguine sun which was slowly going down and started to immerse its great color in the calm waters of the sea.

I only remembered that it was sometime back when my finger touched her finger while walking on the beach but never realized when our palms came together while walking and talking about the scenic beauty and our own life. When both of us realized that we are still holding our hands together then at one moment we might have thought to pull out, but we never did so. Perhaps both of us enjoyed the feeling and the coziness of the warmth and security that we felt with each other.

Now after the entire day of travel and fun we still were full of thrill and energy although never bothered to think whether the source of energy was from the beautiful scenic places of Vizag or from the adorable company of one another that we were enjoying. It was time to retire to hotel as she had to do her packing to board her train, early next morning. Also I did not want her to miss her dinner with her friends and batch mates as she might have missed their presence throughout the day.

I dropped her at her hotel and bid her goodbye after this lovely trip with all the emotions of gratitude that I felt for being with her for the last 3 days and took a commitment from her that we would meet again soon.

I started walking down to my hotel and it was almost a 10 min walk from there. I was really happy and thankful to the Almighty for those lovely moments that I had enjoyed for the past 3 days and was feeling as if this was the end of my first ever planned unofficial tour where I travelled to discover a purpose that I believed in.

Now a strange thought also grabbed my mind that in this entire 3 days' time we never talked or thought about Anisha for a single time. Suddenly out of nowhere it started pouring heavily and now I believe that things do not always go the way you expect them to be.

I took a lane away from the main street with a hope to protect myself form the rain with some shelter somewhere. But situation worsened and it became completely dark as the electricity went off.

Fortunately I could find one gate open and without thinking for a moment I entered the premises and never bothered to interpret the meaning of the sign "Beware of Dogs". I got up onto the portico to save myself from being further drenched by rain. I found the front door of the house locked. About 3 minutes from then I started feeling discomfort as it was not the way anyone should enter the premises of someone on a dark night which is rainy and stormy especially when you are new to the place and not aware about the language with all sorts of strange noises ringing your eardrums which leave you blank regarding the meaning of those words.

Suddenly a light flashed on me as a black car entered the premises of the house with its headlights on. I felt as if I was a specimen drenched in rain and being observed under a microscope. I expected the light would go off in a moment and was desperately waiting for that moment to come which indeed never arrived. Now, a door towards the driver's side opened and I could see a feminine figure coming out of the car but was unable to see her face since the headlights of the car were blinding me. All that I could see is a lady approaching me with a slow gait and the rain drops that touched my skin after being drifted away by the windy breeze gave me goose bumps.

She came in front of me and stood right in front of my eye balls blocking the passage of the beam of light falling on my face and now what I saw seems to be totally manipulated and unpredictable and I never knew how to react to that situation.

She was Anisha with all her grace and smiling at me just as a kid smiles when caught by her mother while doing some mischief. I still did not react – No emotions- No fear – No feelings.

She caught me by my arm and I could feel her freezing chilled hands giving a sense of chillness that passed down my spine on her touching me. She grabbed my arm in her right hand and pushed the shut door with her left hand and then dragged me inside. She left my hand when I found myself inside the mysterious room where I was unable to see anything in the dark and hence stood still. Then suddenly with a flash of light from a match stick she lighted a candle. She went slowly up to the door and shut it while the head-lights of her car were still on.

Now she came close to me, looked at me and smiled again.

With a soft and calm authoritative voice contradicting the outside noise of rain she said 'Are you afraid of me Sneh? You were happy with me when you did not know me well. Now that you know me well you seems to be scared of me! Should we always remain stranger to each other to be happy?'

I stood still for a while. I did not remember about the last time, when I spoke anything. But now I finally mustered all my courage and asked 'Do you intend to kill me?'

She laughed and then paused with her charismatic smile. Then said 'I always have loved you and want to love you more. I don't even believe that I would ever say this to you any day. But this is true which has kept all my desires and wishes alive even long after I am gone.'

Now I felt as if someone is speaking to me as a friend rather that someone who does not exist.

So I started speaking to her as a friend and said 'I came to know all about you and your feelings from Aakanksha.'

'Did she share all that I felt for you?'

'Yes she did.'

Anisha looking deep into my eyes said 'At least she told you how much I loved you which I guess I could have never done myself.'

I asked 'Do you still love me?'

She answered my question with a question, 'Do you feel love is time bound? It is a feeling which once aroused for someone continues for ever. It is only up to us whether we realize it or not in every moment.'

'Should I be scared if I say I am in love with Aakanksha?'

With a sudden gush of wind one of the windows flanged open.

Anisha asked me 'Would you mind shutting the window pane?'

I turned around and walked up to the window and as soon as I pushed the window pane against the wind to shut it, there was light everywhere as if the electricity is back. I turned around quickly but there was no trace of Anisha.

I dared not calling her name again and slowly walked towards the door. As I opened the door I found myself outside the entrance, within the premises of the hotel where I had dropped Aakanksha about 20 minutes back. There was no rain, no car, and no headlights to support what I had been through for the past few minutes. I looked at my watch and was shocked to see that it had been only 1 minute since I wished goodnight to Aakanksha.

I quietly walked down to my hotel and made up my mind not to speak anything regarding this to Aakanksha at least till she reaches Vadodara. Next morning I boarded my train and started preparing myself psychologically to get back to work after this journey which was totally a different experience all together.

Liquid Test Of Love

After a busy week of work it was Saturday again and I remembered that I had not spoken to Aakanksha for a week now although I remembered her every now and then. I called her up and was happy to know that she was anxiously waiting for my call. But now I find some kind of restlessness in her voice. She spoke to me about her dreams in which Anisha comes throughout the week and laughs at her saying satirically 'we had shared our feelings, our heart but not the person who occupies our heart.'

Now both of us were sure that this was not a dream neither for Aakanksha nor for me although both of us were going through something unnatural and unrealistic. Before asking anything else, I raised a question to Aakanksha out of my own curiosity.

'So what kind of feeling do you have regarding me in your heart?'

I was not sure about "What" a girl would answer to that but was sure enough about "How" a girl would respond. She responded in a known fashion as anticipated from a girl when poised with such a question.

'I definitely have some feeling for you although not sure what name I can give to it.'

After listening to the answer as anticipated, I said 'I respect your feelings and words but would definitely give you more time to identify this feeling. I am in Delhi next week. Will it be possible for you to meet me there?'

'I am going home next week but can plan to meet you there before proceeding for home.'

I told her my plan, 'I will be reaching Delhi on Wednesday and will be there till Friday. When can you plan to join me there?'

She said 'In that case, I will meet you on Friday. Make sure that you stay back on Friday.'

'Not again. How many times do I have to reschedule my tickets?' (I whispered to myself.)

'What?' She asked as if she heard it right.

'Nothing. My boss was trying to reach me over the phone.' (To self – guess she might understand what made me said that.)

'So we are meeting at 5 PM on next Friday.'

'At India Gate.'

I didn't know what made me say that, but may be because India Gate is the most prominent epitome or symbol that comes to my mind when I think of Delhi. Aakanksha was fine with the proposal and I started preparing in my mind as I decided to discuss all the things that happened between Anisha and me.

It was Saturday and exactly one week from now I would be meeting Aakanksha. Now that I knew when we were meeting it looked as if the days were very long and nights even longer and doesn't pass with ease. Saturday looked long and Sunday looked longer. This time I really had to say 'Thank God, It's Monday.' I wished my boss or my HR would have heard that and nominated me for a rapid recognition award.

I booked my tickets for New Delhi and was prepared to depart on Tuesday.

After coming back from office on Monday evening, I went to Empress Mall to purchase something for Aakanksha. I had nothing in mind as to what I should get her. I went for a dress and when I entered a boutique on the first floor, a sales girl approached me asking 'Are you Mr. Snehashish?'

I was taken by surprise and before I could ask anything regarding this she pointed out to a violet color dress and said 'A lady who picked up this dress had asked me to keep this dress especially for you as you are looking forward to gift this to someone very special for you and the person gifted would definitely admire this as she loves this color."

'Who was she? Did you ask her name?'

'No sir. She just left a note for you' replied the sales girl.

When I saw the note, it said, 'Dear Sneh, someone who likes you in life will always like this dress too.'

I didn't know who she was as there was no name mentioned on it. But I was scared to give in to my fears which slowly started swallowing my belief as I had read this handwriting before and it resembled much that of Anisha since I had gone through all her letters that she had written to me earlier. Also she had addressed the note on the name "Sneh" which she normally calls me even in letters. I was scared enough to take this dress but also liked it very much by visualizing Aakanksha in it.

Anyway I had to take some dress and this seemed to be one of the finest dresses in the boutique, although I did not go for a treasure hunt in the boutique. The best thing was it saved my effort in choosing a women-wear which I believe is amongst one of the hardest job on this planet.

So I picked it up and asked for wrapping it up as a gift. I went back to my room, packed my luggage and also the baggage of incidents that I thought I would discuss with Aakanksha about Anisha.

I boarded the train on Tuesday so that I can comfortably attend my training scheduled on Wednesday and Thursday. Then came Friday and I had to undergo a driving test as per my company policy and believe me, it was not just another test but a test tougher than qualifying for my job interview. This test is to be taken by an Austrian company which is paid to disqualify employees like us based on minute mistakes. I cannot manipulate the outcome of this driving test but one thing I did was lied the agency by saying 'I have to board an early train and hence will have to complete the test by 2 PM'. The trainer agreed to it and I became free by 2 PM.

Then I had a sumptuous meal as I relish Delhi food very much since it is a blend of various cuisines especially a lot of influence from Punjabi dishes. I took a bus ride to India Gate but this time remembered to collect the ticket on my own from the conductor sitting at one place because I remember once being penalized earlier in Delhi for anticipating the conductor to come to me to hand over the ticket.

When I got down from the bus I was happy and enthusiastic to see in front of me the huge amazing piece of Architecture of History of India- "India Gate". Then I looked at my watch and it revealed that I am 20 minutes before the scheduled time. I was fortunate enough that I did not have to wait for long as Aakanksha also reached 5 minutes after me.

Now I never wanted to go into the analysis of finding the reason behind both of us reaching early whether be it our ego to prove that the other one was late or it was our own desperation to reach there to meet each other. No time for all this. What I can see is now a girl looking more beautiful and attractive than ever. It might have been difficult to decide for ages whether someone looks more beautiful when in love or as is said beauty lies in the eyes of the beholder and it looks more and more charming when you plunge deeper in love.

Sometimes we get strange feeling which is difficult to identify and define such as I was feeling proud of her being so beautiful and at the same time was feeling insecure of her being so attractive. I decided to go for the simplest decision – use the heart not the mind- enjoy the present and no to do any analysis.

We moved around together throughout the beautiful landscape of "India Gate" and settled down near the bank of the water body with ice-cream cones in our hand. Ice cream is having a perfect blend of flavor and chillness just like the chemistry of emotions and love blended together. But one irony is when you start to love someone, you offer ice-cream but when you are married and bound to love someone you ask him/her to cut down on ice-cream in concern for their health. So does it mean that we are not concerned for someone's health when we are newly in love with that person?

As we settled down we both were preoccupied with multiple feelings and emotions and were unable to speak as we used to do earlier. We were even wondering how and where to begin our conversation when suddenly someone intervened and helped us. 'Such a beautiful Jodi; may God bless you.' We turned around and saw it was an eunuch asking for money. I took out a Rs 10 currency note from my wallet and handed it over to the gracious cupid.

The eunuch blessed us again and left us with an assurance not to disturb again.

Aakanksha was prompt enough to ask, 'why did you handover the money? Only because someone appreciated the Jodi!'

'No, not for that. But indeed the comment was not bad.'

Aakanksha replied slowly looking down at the water 'But I am not sure if I am actually in love with you.'

I proposed a trial to prove it and said 'There is one way to test it out and you can actually get a confirmed result if you want to try it now.'

'And how is that?'

'Let's take out our shoes and sit near the water by dipping our legs up to just below our knees in the water. Just wait, relax and forget. You will come to know the results in sometime.'

We did as per what I said. Then I started narrating all the incidents that happened to me in connection with Anisha. Aakanksha also narrated few incidents in which she felt the presence of Anisha by her side. It was quite clear from the incidents narrated by each one of us that we were not alone in what was happening between us but there is someone else along with us who has brought us together and follows us all the time since sometime.

One incident which she narrated was that, once when she was all alone in her room on the evening of my birthday and both of us were talking to each other over the phone, suddenly the call dropped and my electricity went off. I thought there was no way to connect Aakanksha again and hence went to sleep. But at that moment strange things continued at Aakanksha's end.

After my phone got disconnected she got a bang on her door along with the doorbell sound. Although she could feel the presence of Anisha but she mustered all her courage to go near the door and asked 'Who is it?'

Then she heard the sound of the bangles and payal and it was the similar sound that she heard few minutes back while speaking to me from the other side of the telephone.

When she tried to peep through the magic eye of the door, she could only see a blurred figurine standing before the door. It seemed as if standing quite close to the door and even after wiping the lens on the magic eye, she could not figure out her face.

So Aakanksha asked again 'Who is it?' but this time a bit louder.

Still no response.

Aakanksha did not dare to open the door and hence she came back quickly on to her bed and as she was about to cover herself up after lying down on her bed, she received a call from Anisha's number which was no more in use since the time she vanished.

Aakanksha anyhow managed to control her fear and picked up the call.

'Have you wished Sneh on my behalf?'

On hearing this sentence in the voice of Anisha, Aakanksha immediately dropped her phone and the call got disconnected and the battery got separated on falling to the ground.

Aakanksha could not sleep the whole night on that day. Now these incidents prove that I was not the only person who felt the presence of Anisha but even Aakanksha was also feeling Anisha's presence by her side from time to time whenever she came close to me.

While discussing all these incidents we suddenly noticed one thing which I anticipated earlier to prove that both Aakanksha and I were in love with each other.

I (pointing to our feet) asked 'so what do you say now about your doubt of being not in love with me? Do you see that both of us have moved our feet towards each other under the water and now touching one another although they were about a yard apart? More importantly we have moved our feet towards one another without realizing that we have done so. This is what I say – "**Liquid test of Love**".'

I can clearly see the blush on Aakanksha's face and she was not trying to look into my eyes anymore while nodding her head. She even did not withdrew her feet from mine thereby expressing her emotional consent to be with me.

Now everything was as clear as the water under our feet; Firstly Aakanksha and me, we both were in love with each other. Secondly Anisha was in love with me although I was not aware about it. And the third thing is that although Anisha is no more but both Aakanksha and I could feel her presence around us and she was the reason who brought us together.

I could not have got a better chance to propose her. I just took her right palm in both my arms and said,

'I Love you Aakanksha.'

Everyone wishes to do something different and say somewhat different and unique when they would be in love and propose someone. But the irony is that, words become immaterial when we love and propose and it is only the feeling that is expressed.

I think the person who would have used these 3 magical words – "I love You" for the first time ever would have been a very wise man or woman as no one else discovered any more powerful combination of words to express this intense feeling which is very strong when nascent and although expressed through these over-used 3 words but always give a sense of newness in feeling.

Aakanksha could not overpower her blushing and could not look into my eyes that evening but whispered in a soft voice 'I love you too.'

We kept sitting there with our legs dipped in water and did not keep a watch on the time. Slowly she rested her head on my shoulder which bolstered a sense of pride and responsibility in me. Both of us were determined to skip our dinner. Pauses were lengthier than the conversations. Suddenly we observed a Delhi police patrol vehicle stopping nearby and a cop approaching us.

On coming near us he asked in a hoarse voice 'What are you up to? Go home; it is 11:30 PM.'

Till that time none of us had looked at our mobile or watch for the time. The great philosopher Albert Einstein had aptly said: *"Put your hand on a hot stove for a minute, and it seems like an hour. Sit with a pretty girl for an hour, and it seems like a minute. That's relativity."*

We got up, gave the cop a nodding assurance and started wiping our feet with our kerchief before putting on our shoes. Just then I remembered that I had bought in a present for Aakanksha. I handed over the gift wrap to her which contained the dress that I had purchased through the strange process of selection.

She was about to open the gift wrap when I asked her 'Let's go from here'; as the cop was still staring at us with a mix of curiosity, impatience and amusement.

We got up from there and walked away from the site after giving a final glimpse at the magnificent India Gate.

Delhi Auto-rickshaws are always there whenever and wherever you need them, but now we had the privilege of a Delhi Cop escorting us to an Auto-rickshaw so that he would never dare to cheat or trouble us in any way. The Auto-rickshaw dropped us in front of the hotel gate where Aakanksha stayed.

After entering the lobby of the hotel, I asked her 'You may now open the present.'

She was eagerly waiting for the moment and she did it. I could see the brilliant smile on her face as she yelled 'This is my favorite color and I love this dress.'

This is just what I was expecting not because of the confidence on my choice but because of what happened when I went out to purchase something for her. This was the last piece of the story which I was supposed to share, but deliberately I decided not to tell her as she might find herself uncomfortable in getting into it. Hence I just stood still and enjoyed her delight. It was time to say Good Night and Good Bye as the huge pendulum clock hung on the wall of the reception rang once diverting our attention to the time which was then 12:30 AM. We did not take much time to depart as now we know very well that no one can separate us anymore. I was preoccupied in all my senses, thought and mind about Aakanksha and no entity in this universe could have disturbed me on that day.

Aakanksha left for her home next morning and asked me not to see her at the railway station as I would be reaching my hotel almost by 1 AM.

I went back next evening to my head-quarter and got myself busy in work, but with Aakanksha always on the wallpaper of my laptop screen.

Surprises –Pleasant Or Strange?

Aakanksha used to call me regularly although I called her whenever I was free from my official workload and mostly on Friday and Saturday in the evening hours. About a month passed and we always spoke to one another on every Friday and Saturday evening.

One Saturday evening while I was preparing to have my dinner, I received a call from Aakanksha asking me about how am I feeling about my finger now. I was stunned to hear this because the previous Friday evening, I had terribly pierced the knife into one of my fingers while trying to chop a mango before dinner. As my palm was aching severely due to the cut I could not call Aakanksha that day. Hence I asked her surprisingly 'How did you come to know about it?'

To my question, Aakanksha replied 'You only had sent me a text saying that you cannot call me as you had cut your finger while trying to chop a mango.'

'Then how did I type the text? I believe typing a text would have been more painful than calling you.'

She too got shocked on hearing this and became more anxious when she searched her entire inbox but could not locate the text. We both were able to understand the mystery to some extent at our own end but remained silent.

Aakanksha slowly whispered 'She not only hears us but watches us too.' I understood what she meant to say. So just said 'Yes' then wished her Good Night and asked her not to worry much about this. Then I disconnected my phone.

Aakanksha went to bed and was trying hard to sleep when she heard her phone ringing. When she lifted her mobile phone she got scared to find Anisha's number calling. It had happened once earlier on my birth day. She did not answer.

The call came for the second time and it was from the same number which she had saved when Anisha was alive but never deleted after she was gone. She even did not answer for the second time. But now she switched it off.

The call came for the third time for her astonishment. She took off the battery but still the call continued.

Finally she mustered all her courage to answer the call. When Aakanksha pressed the answer button then a voice said 'Hi….. Don't be afraid of me. I love you so much as I did earlier. I also love Sneh even today as I did in those times. But no need to tell you as no one knows my feelings better than you.'

'But you are no more with us!'

Voice from the phone whispered 'That does not change anything between either of us. End of material body is not the end of emotions. It does not require only a body to exist to contain or transmit emotions. Thanks for sharing my emotions to Sneh through my letters. You did a great favor to me and did that thing which I could never have been able to do it myself. Now he understands me well. I will take him with me forever.'

'No, Please don't.'

Voice form the Phone started laughing as its loudness increased 'He he he ……'

The voice was really scary for Aakanksha and now she got up from her bed with the phone in hand and opened the door, went out of her room and knocked on the door next to her room to relieve herself from the fear although she was not quite sure as to what she was doing.

As soon as the door opened the phone got disconnected.

Dipanwita standing at the other end of the door asked, 'Hi, What is it?'

'My phone doesn't work.' Since now she has nothing to show and nobody would believe in whatever she tells.

Dipanwita replied in a casual voice, 'Arey stupid, there is no battery inside. How do you expect it to work?'

'Oh yes. Sorry. Good night.'

'Good night. Have some sleep.'

Aakanksha went back to her bed in her room but never dared to put back the battery in the mobile phone. She and only she would be able to say if she could sleep that night.

In the meanwhile a few projects of global Sustainability came along my way. No need to mention that these kept me on my toes. I had to ignore repeated calls from Aakanksha as I used to be in meetings during those calls. Only I could text her to call back but never kept my word as I had to drive home late after the hectic schedule.

It was really harsh on my part not to call her back again. One fine morning I realized that I had done most of the task assigned to me by my global Sustainability colleagues and was having at least 20 days in hand before they revert again. Also I realized that it was Saturday and I should call her immediately to patch up the wrong that I had done.

I jumped off my bed to reach out to my phone and called her number. But before my call could ring a bell in her phone, someone ranged my doorbell. Although I got irritated but had to disconnect my phone and went towards the door to open it.

As I glanced through the magic eye on the door, I could not believe my eyes to see the person whom I was calling on the phone is standing on the other side of my front door.

It was Aakanksha.

I opened the door.

Aakanksha hurriedly entered my flat and said 'I will kill you; and I mean it. What takes you so long to open the door?'

I did not have any word to argue. Nor had the intention to do so. If eyes would have been the weapons I would have been dead long ago. Words would not have been enough that day and even meaningless before her.

I tried to pacify her by saying, 'Hey, give me 5 minutes as I just woke up.'

'No. You are still sleeping. I won't let you wake up. Go, take 30 Minutes and get ready. Let's go out as I cannot stay for long in this shabby bachelor's apartment.'

I smiled and told her (Putting the TV on) 'Make yourself comfortable.'

'30 minutes. Don't be late.'

I rushed and was ready in about 45 minutes. I assumed she won't mind the delay as I followed IST-"Indian Stretchable Time". Although she pretended to be annoyed but her eyes emitted more shades of love than anger.

We both went out around 9:30 AM and since this was not an ideal time for movie, mall or a park, I proposed to go to a temple. Nearby there was a Shirdi Sai Baba temple which was of great eminence for the people of Nagpur and is on the Nagpur-Wardha highway on the way to the airport. But surprisingly this would have been the first instance where I saw her reluctance and denial to go to a temple. It was not only her reluctance that I gazed on her face but also a bit of fear in her eyes as if she had committed some sin.

Hence I asked 'What is it? What makes you uncomfortable?'

'Naa Sneh. Let's go somewhere out of the city.'

I was a bit surprised as Aakanksha never used to call me by the name "Sneh". She had always called me "Ashish". But later thought this might be due to the reason as whenever you are in love you always try many names to address your love.

The only place that came to my mind where you can go out of the city and is nearby is "Ramtek".

Then I said 'Okay. Let's drive out of the city.'

As I started with Ramtek in my mind she asked me 'Please do not take me to any more temples as I don't want to focus or talk with anyone else other than you; not even God.' I said 'Fine' as I knew that Ramtek would provide us enough things to see and do apart from the ancient temple which is a place to mark the presence of Ram and his brother Laxman during the days of their exile.

This was a very short trip but long enough to observe a lot of changes in Aakanksha since I last met her in Delhi. I saw her inclination towards melodies of Black & White movies of the golden era of "Devanand" which she insisted to play on my FM. Strange but fortunate that all her favorite track were on FM on that day. Earlier as I remembered Aakanksha used to be a great fan of "Kishor da" and her favorite songs were from the movies of romantic 70s of the first super hero Rajesh Khanna.

Tastes may change from time to time hence I thought not to ask anything on this. On the way we stopped to pick up few packets of chips and she also grabbed a bottle of coke although she never was in a habit of consuming any aerated drink earlier.

On reaching Ramtek she gave me the most stunning surprise when she offered to drive on the hilly terrain herself. This was a surprise which I could not digest with ease as Aakanksha never knew how to drive about a fortnight ago and now she is confident enough to drive on the arduous turning of a hill which requires a lot of skill and expertise to play with clutch, gear and brake at the same time.

However I was not confident enough to handover the wheels. She laughed and asked 'Do you still believe that I would kill you?'

I did not understand the meaning of the word "still" as I thought this is the first instance of risking our lives together.

My curiosity and anxiousness reflecting on my face was good enough for her to guess what was running through my mind. She only kept smiling and said nothing more. I reached the hill top of Ramtek but since she was determined enough not to enter into any temple premises, I drove down straight towards the lake. On reaching the lake, she insisted for boating and we took a double paddle boat. Paddling to the middle of water is always a delight for the people who are newly in love as they feel they are now insulated from all the other creatures of the society who are on land and no one can hear them anymore. But for many people like us, words deny coming out of our lips and mind wanders without any thread of connection.

After reaching somewhat in the middle of the lake she whispered me asking not to paddle anymore. I did so and so she did. We had paid to roam throughout the lake in all directions but her words disturbed me once again as she said 'Why wander directionless unless you know where to go.'

I tried not to decipher any meaning out of it and simply asked her to explain.

She took my arms in her arm and I found her arms to be freezing chilled as ice. Then she asked me 'Do you love someone who loved you forever till her end and beyond or would love someone who started after all it ended?'

Confusingly I asked 'Please be clear as I do not follow anything that you intend to say.'

'Should you love Anisha or Aakanksha?'

'Love is not something that is to be logically thought of or a decision. It is rather a foolish accident that we encounter in life.'

I gave a sarcastic smile to compliment what I said. To justify what I just said I added one more sentence to it. 'Love is not about whom we chose to be with. It is all about what or how we react when we are in a situation like this.'

She smiled and said 'You are still not ready. Let's go back to the shore.'

I recollected the words of Anisha at Chikaldara which echoed in a similar fashion 'You are still not ready.'

Slowly we paddled back to the shore. We had a good time at Ramtek looking at the beautiful landscape of the hills, and lake at the sunset.

Journey For The Quest Of Origin

It was time to go back to Nagpur and we started on our journey back. I asked Aakanksha as to what are her next plans and she said 'Chipilima.'

My reaction was very prompt and spontaneous. 'What?'

Aakanksha replied in a soft but grave voice. 'It is my birth place. Let's go there and complete the cycle of existence.'

But now I remember my interaction with Aakanksha in the university Lawn at Vadodara where she told me that she was born and brought up at Hyderabad.

Hence I asked, 'But you said that you were born at Hyderabad!'

'Oh did I? I never remember saying that. My hometown where I was born, started toddling and started my first school was in Chipilima – a small but beautiful place close to Sambalpur.'

'But why do you intend to go there? Do you have someone staying there?'

'It is the place where the journey started and an ideal place to end the journey.'

'You are becoming more and more mysterious in your words and actions compared to my Aakanksha whom I thought I knew so well.'

'It is always better to love someone you know than to know someone you love. At least you won't get undesirable surprises.'

'OMG! You sound so confusing. When do you wish to go?'

Aakanksha immediately replied without a second of delay, 'Let's start tonight and reach tomorrow.'

'How is it possible? I haven't yet booked any tickets. Moreover there is only one train which departs from Nagpur tomorrow afternoon at 2 PM and reaches Sambalpur at around midnight on the same day. It is not only hard but also next to impossible to get a confirmation in the same evening when the train is about to start from Lokmanya Tilak Terminus (LTT) in Mumbai.'

'Book that, it will be confirmed. I can assure you.'

'Shall I book a room for you at Hotel Prime International or would you choose to share a room with one of my junior "Sanskrita" who is now pursuing her Masters in Agriculture at College of Agriculture, Nagpur?'

'Book me in Prime International. Your junior would never be comfortable with my presence in her room, even if I don't share anything with her.'

I booked her in the hotel next to the airport. We reached the hotel in Nagpur at around 8:30 PM and went straight to the "Dhaba" restaurant where we had a sumptuous dinner.

Then I asked her 'So what time shall I meet you tomorrow?'

'I will meet you directly at the Railway station.'

'Strange, but fine.'

I thought not to ask her what she would be doing next morning as I believed she was tired enough to wake up late next morning and may be thinking to relax by the pool side. My first action on going back to my room was to immediately apply for a 2 days of leave for the coming Monday and Tuesday. Also left a note of apology to my boss for such a short notice. Hope he understands the unplanned urgency in a bachelor's life which he might have also been through during his days.

Then I booked 2 waitlisted tickets for Aakanksha and myself up to Sambalpur with 51 and 52 on the waitlist with a hopeless meagre chance to confirm. Totally hopeless about the confirmation part of those tickets, I called Prime hotel and informed them of a possible extension of stay for Aakanksha.

Saturday evening has always been special for me as I watch late night movies without worrying to wake up early next morning for the office. Right from my college days I love going to bed quite late on Saturday night and waking up quite late on lazy Sunday morning. I still remember during my B-school days where we had a gang that would wake up around 12 noon on Sunday only to relish the chicken Biryani being served in our hostel and then again go back to bed to complete the second innings of our sleep in the afternoon.

This Saturday would have been different had I committed Aakanksha to meet next morning. I switched on my idiot box and was fortunate enough to find a horror movie which I always love to watch in a perfectly scary ambience. As I stretched my legs on my sofa with a diet coke in my hand after switching off the drawing room lights to enjoy my horror movie in a theatre style, I suddenly felt somebody's presence by my side. I sat upright for some time and then switched on the light for a better feel. I would not hesitate to say that I was a bit scared but was sure that it was not the effect of the movie.

After few minutes when I switched off the lights and returned back to the sofa I could not find my Cola can by my side. Again I switched on the lights but could not find it anywhere in the drawing room. Finally I traced it back to the top of my refrigerator in the kitchen but was shocked to see it there as I do not remember going back to the kitchen once I have taken the Cola can out of the refrigerator. I kept the lights on and watched the movie although things outside the TV kept on bugging me.

Finally it was 1 AM when I decided to switch off my TV set and retire to bed for the day. I switched off all the lights and went to sleep. I did not know how much time had passed but heard as if Anisha is whispering my name in my ears. It was the very same voice which I encountered when I was in Vizag.

Suddenly I woke up but found no one near me. But was more shocked to see all the lights were on, although I firmly remember myself switching off all the lights before going to bed. Although I was not scared but felt a bit uncomfortable and decided to switch off only my bed room lights while the drawing room lights were still on.

Next morning on waking up I found all the lights were switched off. I still could not believe it as I clearly remember what I did that night.

I did not know what to do in the morning as Aakanksha told me to meet only at the Nagpur Railway station. So I picked up my phone to give her a ring but could not find any network in it. It was really strange as I had been observing this phenomenon since yesterday that my phone is only showing network when Aakanksha was around but since she was there, there was no need to call her up. But when I felt the need to call her up there was no network. Switched off and switched on several times but still no display of network, only SOS.

Still hopeless but yet started packing my bag for an unknown journey. Could not inform anyone as there was no network in my phone. At 12 Noon I thought of checking the fate of those waitlisted tickets and was surprised to find them confirmed as the chart had been prepared. Now actually for the first time ever I became psychologically prepared for the journey. I had my lunch in a nearby mess and reached the station by 1:15 PM.

As I took out my phone to call Aakanksha with a hope to find network, I actually found full network which tempted me to think that might be she is around. I was indeed right as she was standing just a few steps ahead of me. 'Are you the mobile tower?' I murmured to her but only in my mind.

She was wearing a big gracious smile on her face and said nothing. We both approached each other and on coming close to me she caught my arm and said 'Let me take you on the final journey where destination meets destiny and life transforms into memory.'

Although surprised and confused since the previous day, I said nothing and kept mum.

She never asked me if the tickets got confirmed but only asked which berths as if she was one among the racket members who operates the railway black reservation business.

Now this was the first time I was travelling with Aakanksha although I had met her several times in different cities. When we entered the train we found a lady who was sitting in our compartment and looked pretty different with her stone necklace and a big black "bindi" on her forehead. She also looked very curious when Aakanksha and I were talking to each other. I asked her about her destination but she said nothing, not even smiled. I thought of asking her again as I felt she might not have heard my question. But this time Aakanksha grabbed my palm and pressed it as an indication for me not to ask anything else.

About an hour passed while talking to one another since the train started from Nagpur Railway station. Aakanksha got up and proceeded for the washroom. Then this strange looking lady sitting in our compartment hurriedly approached me and asked 'Are you sure, you are going for this journey? I don't think you are ready for it.'

Before I could speak up anything to her, Aakanksha entered the compartment and on seeing her, this lady hurriedly left for the washroom.

I asked Aakanksha, 'Hey, you are back so soon?'

'Just to spy on you for what are you conspiring in my absence' she said smilingly.

She again picked up her hand bag and went for the washroom. It might not have been a couple of minutes after Aakanksha left for the washroom, we heard a loud scream and rushed to see what happened with all sorts of negative assumptions coming to mind. I was really worried about Aakanksha since she was the last one to leave for washroom.

We were shocked to see this strange looking lady in a pool of blood with blood oozing out from her neck and shoulder. Fortunately we had the TTE in our coach and he also rushed to the scene hearing the loud scream.

On asking what really happened, this lady only said 'Please let me go off this train and see a doctor.' Although she said this loud but she was only staring at Aakanksha as if she was pleading Aakanksha with fear to let her go off the train. The TTE made arrangements for her and she got down at a small station in the next 10 minutes where there was a doctor waiting for her as intimated by the TTE. We wished her a speedy recovery but she said nothing and only looked at Aakanksha with scary eyes.

No one on that train that day would be able to tell accurately what happened to her although people kept on discussing and guessing for hours together.

When I was saying, 'She was shocked and scared as if she had seen a ......'

'Ghost', Aakanksha interrupted smilingly.

'Exactly.'

'And now you might be thinking that I am the ghost who did this to her.'

'No, but you were the only one who left from the compartment after her. I mean...... No...'

Aakanksha again interrupted 'yeah that's what I am saying. I am a ghost who did this to her. Are you scared now?' Then she gave a rich and luring smile to strengthen what she had said.

'Come on. Let's change the topic. Talk about something else.'

As the evening hours drew near Aakanksha only looked out of the window and on asking what was going on in her mind, she said 'I wish we would have travelled the whole night just sitting close and talking to each other as we did earlier.'

I reminded her and said 'Hello Madam, This is our first train journey ever.'

She gave me a very playful look and said 'Really!' I was so confused by her look that I decided not to argue any more with her.

Then I proposed, 'Let's go out and have some fresh air standing near the entrance gate.'

We went out of the compartment and stood near the entrance of the coach. It was a refreshing feeling standing at the gate from being seated in a closed AC coach for the entire day and I started feeling pleasant as my body was slowly acclimatizing to the outside temperature.

Now she asked me a strange question although it is quite familiar one for people newly in love. 'Were you always that sweet or being especially sweet to me?'

I responded it with another question, 'Why do you feel so?'

'Since childhood you have been very sweet but used to talk a lot which you currently do not do.'

'You are saying as if you had been a classmate of mine since childhood. Oh I understand, you must have known me through the eyes of Anisha.'

'Yeah, I have seen you always through the eyes of Anisha. They were my own eyes.'

We stood there looking at the setting sun till it was almost dark and then went inside back to our berths. It was about 10:30 PM when people started unfolding their bedroll and switching off the lights thereby making it perfectly cosy for their sleep in the train at night. I also stood up to do the same but suddenly Aakanksha caught up my wrist and said, 'Let's talk for some time till we reach Sambalpur.'

I thought this to be a better idea as we were supposed to get down at Sambalpur and we were expected to arrive somewhere around 1AM, hence there is always a risk lurking to fall asleep and miss the station at night when the time of arrival is so odd. Fortunately we had a lower berth and so we unfolded our bed roll, switched off the lights and sat close to each other holding hand in hands, looking at the lonely moon out of the window. Her palms were freezing cold. I was about to ask her regarding this, when she stopped me by saying 'Don't speak anything. Just try to live in these wonderful moments and feel them through your soul which you might not get in this world again.'

I could not resist any longer and asked what she meant by these words that she had just spoken.

She replied with a 'Shhhhhh..... Listen to the unspoken silence and enjoy the moments.'

I decided not to disturb her again. She was holding my palms tightly but the more she was holding it tight the more I was feeling the chillness from her hand. Her face was glowing as bright as the snow with the moonlight falling on her cheeks. We kept on sitting hands in hands for about an hour staring at the full moon out of the window in the darkness. I was hopeful of turning her hands warm with my body heat. But finally I could no more bear the chillness of her frozen hands and simply pulled out my arms saying 'It's pretty cold.'

Aakanksha said (without reacting to my pulling of hands) 'You cannot stop the time from fleeing but time doesn't carry me on its wing. I love you the same way as I used to do since many years.'

I thought that she might be feeling as if we are in love since many years, at least not from previous life. Love drives people crazy and I perceived that she was not an exception.

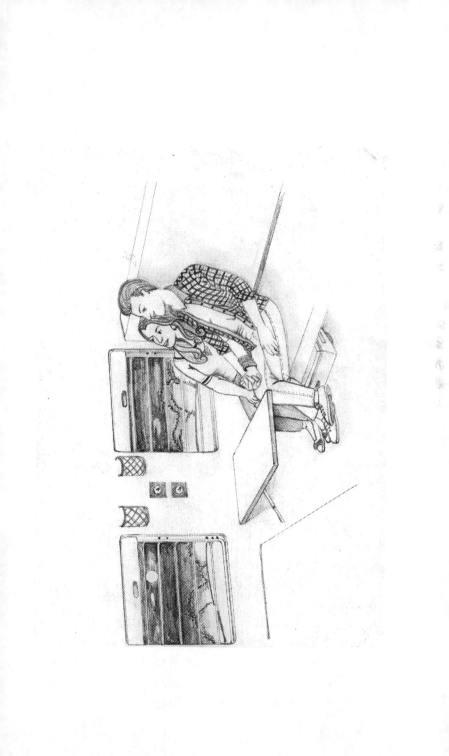

Suddenly my phone rang breaking all the silence. When I took it out from my pocket I was surprised to see that the call was from Aakanksha. Without a moment's delay, Aakanksha snatched the phone out of my palm and disconnected the call saying it might have been dialled due to pressure of her arm on her bag where her phone is lying. As our train arrived in the next station, we realized that we were close to Sambalpur station and then Aakanksha said that she has to go to the washroom.

After she left for the washroom I noticed one thing which added to my confusion and enhanced my curiosity. Her mobile phone was kept on charging mode connected with an adaptor and was far from where Aakanksha was sitting. Hence there was no question of mere pressure being the reason for dialling a call automatically from her mobile phone to mine. I thought of dialling back on Aakanksha's number from where the call came but as I guessed there was no network again.

Our train reached Sambalpur station and came to a halt. I was still waiting for Aakanksha. Then finally went on knocking all the washroom's doors and yelling out her name.

She did not respond. The train was about to leave the platform so I hurriedly pulled out all the bags out of the train onto the platform. Even her mobile phone was now with me. I was really worried looking at the entrance of our coach as the train whistled and started rolling its big circular iron wheels. Now I became more desperate, went near the door and started walking along with the moving train holding one of its long iron handle.

Suddenly an ice cold freezing hand caught me on my shoulder. 'Are you looking for me?'

I turned around and it was Aakanksha.

I was really mad at her when I burst out saying, 'What the hell is this? Do you think it's funny playing with me at around midnight on an unknown station?'

Aakanksha smilingly said, 'I won't leave you here after bringing you so far with me.'

I was really fuming with anger but her charismatic smile had great power to soothe all my anger.

I told her to wait there and said, 'Let me go out and check for a conveyance.'

Leaving her at the waiting room with our bags, I moved out to check for a conveyance. I went up to an Auto-rickshaw parked outside the station, and suddenly I remembered that I forgot to ask Aakanksha for the address. Seeing the network finally on my phone after so long hide and seek with network, I finally dialled on Aakanksha's Number. Aakanksha picked up the call and 'where the hell are you? Do you have any idea regarding how many days have passed since the last time we spoke to each other?'

These words really swallowed my senses up to its root.

'Come-on, I am just outside the railway station and I have told you that I am going to look out for a conveyance. Now tell me your address in Chipilima so that I can negotiate the rate with the Auto-rickshaw driver.'

The voice from the phone asked me, 'Are you at Sambalpur Railway station? With whom?'

'Come on this is not funny anymore. After being with me for the last 2 days and coming with me all this way, you are trying to pull my leg at midnight 1 AM. Don't behave in such a crazy manner.'

'She has brought you this far? Anisha has taken you there.'

'And who are you madam?'

Voice from the phone was really panicking as it said 'I am Aakanksha. Believe me. The one along with you is Anisha. Her parents were from Chipilima. Please stay away from her. Believe me.'

'Why should I believe you?'

'She would go to sector No. 19, Buddha Raja colony, which was her home. Please be careful and stay away from her. I am at Cuttack right now with my parents. Will definitely reach you tomorrow, but till then…..'

The phone got disconnected and suddenly a hand was on my shoulder.

I turned around and it was Aakanksha, who satirically spoke to me. 'I thought you were supposed to call an Auto-rickshaw?'

Really confused, shocked, astonished, perplexed, tired and exhausted at that moment, I somehow managed to say 'Ye…. Ye…. Yes. I am. But where do you want to go?'

'Sector 19, Buddha Raja Colony, Chipilima.'

Was it a prank or some kind of joke or am I exhausted for the day without sleep? (Thought in my mind)

'Did I just call on your mobile?'

'No. Why?'

'Nothing. Let's go.

Auto, Sector 19, Buddha Raja colony, Chipilima.' (Shouting at the Auto-rickshaw driver)

'Rs 400 Sir.' Replied the Auto-rickshaw driver.

I started negotiating 'Rs 300. Nothing more.'

And the bargain continued. 'Rs 380'

'Rs 350 only. That's final. If not then let me try …'

Finally the Auto-rickshaw driver agreed and said 'Okay sir. Come on in.'

Aakanksha and myself, we both boarded the Auto-rickshaw and still I believed what happened over the phone was a prank from Aakanksha. But only thing which I noticed was that she never talked about it nor laughed at it making fun of me.

Another strange thing which drew my attention was that she was so anxiously looking into the dark as if she could clearly see everything outside even though it was pitch black out there. This was a clear emotion which can be observed among people when they return to their places of origin after a long time.

But the strange part was that, she warned the Auto-rickshaw driver to drive safely due to the bad road conditions and was able to tell him in advance regarding the craters on road as if she commutes on that way every day and absolutely familiar about the road condition. The thing which surprised me most was that she once warned the Auto-rickshaw driver to slow down or else he would hurt a deer on the road and about 5 minutes from then the auto driver had to apply sudden brake breaking the silence of the dark night with a loud screeching sound of the skidding rickshaw tyre on the concrete road which almost was about to topple down in an attempt to save a deer which suddenly came before the vehicle.

The driver who was frightened enough, looked at Aakanksha and dared not to utter a single word on this incident. We reached Sector 19, Buddha Raja colony and she pointed out to a house whose lights were still on, whereas rest all houses were sleeping in the darkness of the night.

'Does your parents know that you were coming?'

'I am always with them. You may drop me here near the gate and I will manage from here.'

Without arguing, I did so and wished her good night.

While entering into the gate of the old house she reminded me, 'I will call you tomorrow. Wait for my call for planning the day.'

I watched her going into the premises of the house after entering through the old rusted Iron Gate which opened with a cranking noise.

I asked the Auto rickshaw driver to drop me at a decent and clean hotel with a reasonable price. He nodded and said 'Okay Sir. Let's go to "Hotel Blue Heaven".'

I did not find the name nice and said, 'No. It does not sound decent.'

'How about "Hotel Sai Krishna"?'

'Sounds better. Take me there.'

The Auto-rickshaw driver out of habit started renegotiating. 'Additional Rs 50 Sir.'

'Okay baba. Now let's go.'

I checked in and it was a decent hotel.

Am I Ready Now For
The Last Plunge?

It was a bright fresh morning when I woke up after the sweet morning tweeting and chirping melody of the small birds outside my window pane. It had drizzled in the wee hours of the morning and the fragrance of the first summer shower coming from the soil was really rejuvenating and refreshing.

Sambalpur is a great city of confluence of many cultures from adjoining states of Odisha and even from distant states. It was the city of 'Mata Samleswari'- a divine form of goddess Shakti as well as the city of the mighty dam Hirakud built on the great river Mahanadi.

Since I woke up early in the morning before sunrise, hence I decided to go to Samleswari temple. I tried calling Aakanksha for joining me for "Darshan" but again the same old problem- no network. But now I had options. I called her from the Hotel reception.

As soon as I called her and before I could say 'Hi' or 'Good Morning', she just somehow realized that it was me on the other side and started speaking, 'Hi, I am on my way to Sambalpur. But please keep away from Anisha. She is there to snatch you from me forever.'

'Stop irritating me in the morning. I know you are there with me since last 2 days and you had come with me till Sambalpur. If you are in no mood to go to the temple then it's fine. I will go alone.'

I disconnected the call immediately. Took a quick shower and went to the temple. It is a great site at Samleswari temple. It was about 2 decades since I last visited the temple for "Darshan" with my parents and Grand Parents when I was a kid. After the "Darshan", I decided to meet Aakanksha as I had no more obligations on that day and I had been there only because she wanted me to be there.

I had my mobile phone but of no use. Hence hired an Auto-rickshaw and went to the same address where I had dropped her the previous night. As I made the payment to the Auto-rickshaw driver and turned back, I was shocked to see a house in a dilapidated condition which looked very much perfect and liveable a night before when Aakanksha went in and I watched her going in, waiting from a distance.

I went near the old rusted gate and swung it open with a cranking noise. As I was about to enter the premises, suddenly I felt a warm hand on my shoulder. I turned back and found an old man in his early fifties standing beside me dressed in white and blue checkered shirt, black trousers and a pair of slippers.

'Are you looking for someone my dear?' He asked.

'Sir, I am looking for Aakanksha and if I am not mistaken, I had dropped her here last night.'

'I am sorry to say, but this cannot be the house, young man. You might have been mistaken. No one by the name Aakanksha lived here. In fact no one live here now. This house has been vacant since last one year.'

'How is this possible? I clearly remember this house and also remember her going into it.'

Suddenly I found a bill of a restaurant from Nagpur Railway station from where we had picked up some snacks. This bill was lying inside the gate. I picked it up and showed it to this gentle man saying that I had not been mistaken regarding the house nor regarding Aakanksha.

Now this senior person seems to be a bit confused and said 'I don't know any one by name Aakanksha who lived here. But Mr and Mrs Mishra used to live here with their lovely daughter Anisha. But that's a sad story for such a sweet angel who was really charming, sensitive and darling of all.'

I was really shocked to hear the name "Anisha".

'Why? What happened to her?'

'Mr and Mrs Mishra could not bear the burden of life after their only child Anisha was killed in a car accident. Mrs Mishra lost her psychological balance and after a prolonged treatment, Mr Mishra decided to move onto a new place to escape from the memories of their sweet and only girl hunting them. Since then this house is vacant.'

'Are you sure that Anisha died in the car accident?'

'Yes (with a deep breath). But sometimes people say, she is seen here in this house and was last seen around her birth day last year. Only God know how true is this?'

Now I could relate to what Aakanksha was saying over the phone. Now there are lot of questions again arising in my mind. "Do I need to keep away from Anisha, even her thoughts? No I am not scared." I started an unspoken conversation in mind.

This conversation continued silently in my mind. "But why do I still look forward to meet her again? Have I started loving her after being with her for last 2 days? No, I believed I was with Aakanksha, so how could I love Anisha?"

Now my mind was a total turbine where questions and thoughts keep pouring and churning. I was literally scratching my head with all these questions. Then I suddenly remembered my etiquettes and thanked the elderly man for whatever he has shared and moved on. As I walked a few steps thinking deep into what I was unable to understand, my mobile phone started ringing.

'Hello'

Aakanksha was on the other end and said, 'Hi. I am about to reach Sambalpur Railway station. Where are you now?'

'I…' Phone got disconnected and I could not speak anything else nor could I say where I was or where I was heading to.

When I was just about to call her back, my phone started ringing again and I saw "Aakanksha calling."

'Hey, when are you reaching Sambalpur?'

The voice from the phone said in a teasing tone 'Hello sweetheart. I am in Sambalpur only and I came here along with you yesterday. How can you forget such a lovely and memorable journey all the way, Sneh?'

I understood that this was Anisha.

'Where are you?'

Voice from the phone slowly and calmly said, 'Sneh, I am at my place where you had dropped me last night. Okay now stop probing and get ready to meet me at the front gate of College of Agriculture, Chipilima. I would take you on a final journey which is so wonderful and unending that even time cannot separate us for good.'

Now I got the feeling as if this would be my last journey from where I might never return. But in spite of Aakanksha trying to warn me several times I was still willing to go for this journey. I just don't know what was running through my mind but wanted to put an end to all this. I knew that I love only Aakanksha but do not know what was attracting me and pulling me towards the unchartered path called Anisha. I was no more in a position to bear this game of "Love and Fear" any further. I was ready for the last plunge and face the darkness.

'Yes I will definitely meet you in next 1 hour.'

By then I had made up my mind to take a plunge in the unchartered water but before that I wished I could have spoken to Aakanksha for the last time. But I knew it well that there won't be any network on my mobile handset once this call ends.

Voice from the phone confirmed me again. 'Bye Bye. See you then in 1 Hour.'

Phone got disconnected and I was right. There was no network at all to call or talk to anyone on the phone. I could have tried from someone else's mobile or any nearby Landline phone but at that moment decided not to call anyone.

I took an Auto-rickshaw and asked him to drop me at College of Agriculture, Chipilima.

I reached there in about half an hour as I never wanted to reach my final destination with a delay. As I got down from the Auto-rickshaw the driver asked me, if he would wait for me to return back?

I simply smiled in response to his question. I don't know what he interpreted form my smile, but told me in a relaxed voice, 'I will be here till next 1 hour. If you feel like going back then just give me a ring on this number.'

He called out his number loudly and I typed the number and dialled it and pretended as if I have saved it to call him back on a return journey which I rarely know would occur.

As I moved on slowly towards the gate of the magnificent campus, a soft voice called me 'Sneh.' I turned around and saw a beautiful young lady getting down from an Auto-rickshaw. She was completely dressed in a black long frock bearing a radiant smile on her face as if she is about to achieve her life's ultimate dream.

There was no comparison of her satisfaction reflecting on her face as if a small child have got her toy back and innocent eyes are filled with rich tear of joys and fulfilment.

She was Anisha in disguise of Aakanksha as Aakanksha never liked to be clad in dark colour especially black since she always used to say 'Black colour signifies great secrets.' On the contrary I used to argue always saying that black is an epitome of authority.

Aakanksha (Actually Anisha) kept on smiling at that place waiting for me to walk towards her. I slowly walked towards her with all my senses although I was clearly aware about her identity and what she was up to. I was not under any kind of fear, nor it was any kind of love but it was a curiosity to know how it is all going to end.

She took me by my arm and took me in a direction against the sun. I simply followed her without speaking anything. She called back the Auto-rickshaw by which she had come and we boarded it. She asked the driver to take us to the Dam near the Ghanteswari temple. This is a small dam but with great depth. We got down near the dam and she asked the Auto-rickshaw driver to leave after paying him.

She again caught me by my arm and took me round the dam onto a narrow swinging wooden bridge over the mighty river Mahanadi.

It was a real dangerous bridge swinging at a great height over the mighty Mahanadi. It looked as if this sky walk over the gorgeous deep blue waters is just made of a series of wooden plates held through a string of ropes which would anytime detach to throw you off from all that altitude to the depth of Mahanadi which you can never fathom.

Beyond the bridge was the beautiful temple of Ghanteswari. The name describes it all. It was a popular belief that anyone, whose prayers are answered, returns here and tie a bell at the temple premises as an offering and thanking the good Lord for all Her blessings. Hence the name Ghanteswari- the temple with numerous bells.

While walking hands in hands she asked me 'Do you love me?'

This is probably one of the most asked questions which are bounced most frequently in the whole galaxy not with an intention to know the answer but check the spontaneity of the response which serves as a confirmation for any girl who is in love with someone.

I simply smiled and said nothing. She asked me again but this time she asked a different one 'Have you ever loved Anisha?'

While continuing with this unknown smile I replied 'I never loved Anisha.'

But before she could say anything else, I said 'I also do not love you. I know that you are Anisha.'

Anisha suddenly stopped walking and turned around at me and asked, 'Are you still afraid of me now?'

'I am not afraid of you or else I would not have come this far with you even after knowing who you are.'

Anisha suddenly transformed to her own form. Smiled back at me and said, 'Good. Then come with me. I will take you to somewhere where we will always be together, ***forever and beyond.***'

'No Anisha. I had never loved you. I love only Aakanksha.'

'You know Aakanksha from only last few months and you say you are in love with her. We are known to each other since our school days. And that's pretty long time Sneh.'

I simply said, 'It is not about how many days or how many years. It is all about how much. If you want to ask why, then sorry, I have no answer to it.'

'Is she more beautiful than me?'

'Beauty is a term which can never be compared or else everyone on this planet would have been after only one girl. Beauty is not about a person. It is rather about that moment which you spend with her and live with her. With Aakanksha my moments are beautiful and hence I love her.'

Aakanksha came running onto the bridge.

Aakanksha took a deep breath and then looking at Anisha said, 'I knew, I would find you here Anisha. You know since childhood this used to be your favourite spot. No matter you were happy or upset; you always shared these moments with these waters.'

I was more than happy to see Aakanksha, may be for the last time. But all these time the fear which was miles away from me now suddenly came along with Aakanksha. It was a fear to lose her forever. Hence I warned her not to step any further towards us.

Anisha in a deceitful smilingly manner asked 'How can you say that he loves you and not me?'

Aakanksha replied with a strange but strong example, 'Open your palm by which you have been holding him tightly. If you find a single drop of sweat on it then I should say it is love.'

Anisha opened her palm and we saw no sweat on it.

Anisha again questioned, 'I am no more a living body. How can I perspire?'

'But Ashish is. If he would have loved you the sweat would have been on your palm as well. When you love someone and hold her hands tightly you would definitely find it sweating. That's the proof of true love. Now if you still want to take Ashish along with you forcefully, he would never be yours anymore. You would lose him forever as he would never have any more feelings for you as feelings always develop in this world only although they may continue in your world as well.'

Anisha responded in a low voice. 'Don't say that I survive only on feelings taken from this world of yours. Do you know why have I never come to him before for so long? Because he never thought of me before. For the first time ever after my death he remembered me when he came across someone by the name Nisha in Jorhat. He then tried to remember me by thinking of some silent shy girl sitting in a corner in his class known for her sweet smile and nice dark eyes known by a similar name although he was not able to retrieve my correct name.'

She continued 'When you remember me, I will come closer. You call my name, you can feel me stronger. I survive on thoughts and memories. The more you try not to remember me, the more I will occupy your mind. Now he thinks more and more about me than he thinks of you as he tries to run away from me all the time. So now he is mine and let him go along with me.'

Then I interrupted the conversation between both Cousins by saying 'Okay. Let me close my eyes for next few minutes and if at all I see you Anisha, then take me with you.'

Aakanksha yelled in a frightened tone 'No. 'Please no. You don't have to do this. I don't want to lose you. She has occupied your mind and she is standing next to you. You will only see her when you close your eyes.'

I assured Akanksha and said 'Don't you worry Aakanksha. Have faith in my love and in God.'

Suddenly the sky became very cloudy and dark and the wind started to blow really fast as if it would throw all of us off the swinging bridge into the deep blue waters of the river Mahanadi. I could also see the stagnant water of the reservoir becoming more turbulent with the blowing breeze which now made the water to dance on its tune creating violent waves. The bells of Ghanteswari temple started ringing louder and louder due to the blowing winds.

I closed my eyes and all that I could sense is the ringing of the bells of Ghanteswari temple really loud. All I could see are those beautiful moments that I had spent with Aakanksha, sitting knee deep in water near India gate, holding hands and walking on the Visakhapatnam beach and sitting together on the lawn of ISKON temple at Vadodara. All I could see is Aakanksha's deep gorgeous beautiful eyes, innocent face and its various expressions of confusion, fear, anxiety, thoughtfulness, caring, enviousness and playfulness. She was a perfect picture of a symbol of love.

It is said that the reason for which bells are there in temples is that when struck they produces a vibration of sound waves which cleanse our minds of any negative thoughts like fear, anxiety, worries and curiosity. It brings our wandering mind from space and time and settles it down with calmness and rest for sweet good memories. The sound of bells in temples and churches or the sound of "Azan" in a mosque only fills the mind with beautiful memories that we have lived with or desire to live.

What could have been more effective in this case than numerous bells ringing simultaneously? There were no beginning and no end to it. Only positivity and glorious moments drenched my mind and brimmed my thoughts. I could feel the electric power of energy called 'Love' flowing through my entire body. I felt as if I was standing under a shower of positive energy flowing like pure white milk from my head to toe.

I don't know how much time would have passed when someone shook me up. I opened my eyes and saw it was Aakanksha. No more clouds, no more storm. It was a clear sky with the sun shining bright. No signs of Anisha. Only the bells were still echoing.

Then I asked 'Anisha?'

Aakanksha (Nodding her head) said, 'she is gone, I believe forever. Now she has her answer and she respects it.'

We both walked together to the other end of the bridge holding each other's hand. On crossing the swinging bridge, we went up to the temple and when we left each other's hand to fold our hand before the Lord, our palms were full of sweat. We looked at one another and smiled.

We kneeled down before the good Lord and thanked Her for bringing us more closer and then tied a bell for answering our prayers.

About The Author

Saumendra Kumar Nayak has about a decade old experience in the corporate world in various MNCs and Indian organization and proved his mettle in the areas of Sales, Marketing and Sustainability. He is a certified behavioural trainer and trained various corporates in areas of sales and marketing from customer behaviour orientation point of view. He has been visiting various Management institutes as guest faculty and delivered honorary lectures on subjects of Marketing, Ethics and Sustainability.

An avid traveller by choice and is interested in the local history and legendary stories of the different remote geography that he visits and tries to experience the little explored areas of entire India with an attempt to weave different cultures together in form of storytelling.

Printed in the United States
By Bookmasters